Love Among the Mashed Potatoes

Love Among the Mashed Potatoes

Gregory Mcdonald

Thomas Congdon Books

E.P. DUTTON | NEW YORK

For information contact: E.P. Dutton, 2 Park Avenue,
New York, N.Y. 10016

Library of Congress Cataloging in Publication Data
Mcdonald, Gregory, 1937-
Love among the mashed potatoes.
"Thomas Congdon books."
I. Title.
PZ4.M13473Lo   [PS3563.A278]   813'.5'4   78-2861
ISBN: 0-525-14905-8

Published simultaneously in Canada by Clarke, Irwin & Company
Limited, Toronto and Vancouver

10 9 8 7 6 5 4 3 2 1

First Edition

To Helen Barrett and Tom Congdon

Love Among the Mashed Potatoes

1.

Dear Mark Edwards:

The other day, Tuesday I think it was, when I was putting my daughter's panties away in her drawer (they're beautiful sheer panties, Mark, blue and gold, her school colors, she insisted, all the girls wear them, bikini style, light as a feather, I wish I'd had such things as a girl—in fact, I wish I could wear such things now without looking like a Sumo wrestler) and lo and behold, what did I find? Contraceptive pills!

Jesus, Mary, and Joseph!

She's only thirteen, Mark.

I was alone in the house, of course, so I went into the kitchen and poured myself a stiff one and sat down at the kitchen table with The Things in my hand and said to myself, "What have we here?"

Well, I knew what we had here. A dear little girl gettin' dipped and diddled in the do-do by every dum-dum.

Our precious doll!

By the time she came home from school, saying, "Hi, been drinkin'?," swaying her perfect little ass at me as she peered up and down the refrigerator shelves, I had begun to calm down a little—after all, she is my daughter, and it would be unnatural for a mother not to think good thoughts about her very own daughter!—so I didn't say anything to her except, "Where's your goddamned training bra?"

Mark, I would have taken any answer from her—any! such as, "In the locker room at school," even "Johnny's flying it from the handlebars of his twelve-speed"—any! except the answer she gave me: "I don't know."

"I don't know"!

I shook The Things in her father's face when he came in the door. "Do you know what these things are? Do you know whose they are?"

"Who gave them to her?"

He's a lawyer, Mark.

So now he wants to sue the family doctor who wrote the prescription, and the local drugstore for filling it for her. He keeps screaming, "Couldn't they see she's only thirteen?"

I'm not so sure, myself.

Of course, I do want my daughter to have every opportunity.

A Concerned Mother
(Mrs. D. Bainbridge)

March 25

Dear ME:

This new column is driving me not only bananas, but apples, pears, nuts, and rutabagas as well.

Can you believe a mother writes me describing her thirteen-year-old daughter's panties? Lord love a duck!

When Jim told me his big idea over lunch, a column called DEAR MARK EDWARDS he said, "No reason why all these advice columns should be written by women. I believe in liberation. So who says women are the repository of all earthly wisdom? You've been liberated all your life."

The booze had gotten to my head. I should never, never have more than two martinis at lunch. Especially with Jim Krikorian.

"You've spent enough time on the desk," he said.

The only thing I could think is: This is the perfect way to screw Pamela. Pamela the philm critic. The philigm critic. Wifey.

A column called DEAR MARK EDWARDS.

Even a forty-year-old journalist like myself has his vanity.

Or maybe I should say thirty-nine years old.

The new column sure is giving me weird new thoughts.

Look! I'm even writing letters to myself.

Dear ME!

Dear me, indeed.

I've never kept a journal before. Instead, I've done crossword puzzles and read history.

And then there's this terrible temptation, this need, to write some of these people back—personally.

I've always written people back when they've written me letters!

(After twenty years a journalist, I'm even beginning to use exclamation marks, like my dearly bereft correspondents.)

(And parentheses.)

(Soon I'll even be writing that fabulous, fantastic American word *alot*!)

March 25

Dear Mrs. Bainbridge:

Regarding your letter describing your discovering your thirteen-year-old daughter is on the Pill (and, by the way, thanks for describing her panties to me in such detail; that was refreshing) my advice is very simple.

Make sure the prescription doesn't lapse.

You've been living your fantasies through her long enough already.

Shouldn't she get to live out some of her own?

I mean, it was you who gave her panties in her school colors, right?

What did you expect her to do with them, use them to erase the blackboard?

Why don't you take off a few tons of your own lard, so you can live out some of your own fantasies?

And watch the lonely boozin', babe.

Love Never Faileth,
Mark Edwards

March 23

Dear Mark Edwards:

The oddest thing is happening to me.

Every time I see my husband, I sneeze.

Every time I'm in the room alone with him, I take a sneezing fit.

The odd thing is that the man who really turns me on is the man who cuts the lawns around here. I've never said anything, of course, I just stand in the window in my negligee watching him as he works, with his shirt off, cutting the lawns up and down the street, front yard, back yard, front yard, back yard.

You'd think it would be the sight of him that would make me sneeze, wouldn't you? I mean, with the grass cuttings and all. Sometimes the window is open.

My husband is an insurance executive, Mark, doing quite well, and never exposes himself to dust or grass cuttings or other sneezy things.

Do you think I've developed an allergy to my husband? Should I see a doctor?

Sneezy
(Mrs. Rossi)

March 25

Dear Dopey:

Forget seeing a doctor.

Take a tip from Brontë and pursue in your negligee your Heathcliff on the lawnmoor over the neighborhood yards.

You're probably insured against laceration.

Love Never Faileth,
Mark Edwards

March 22

Dear Mark Edwards:

It sure is nice having a man write one of these columns. That's all I have to say. It sure is nice having a man write one of these columns.

Spike

March 23

Dear Mark Edwards:

I'm fourteen and I really like masturbating alot.
But everybody tells me it gives me pimples.
I don't have many pimples.
But will it give me pimples?
I really like masturbating.

Jerry Jerk-off

March 25

Dear Jerry Jerk-off:

Masturbating doesn't make pimples.

In fact, jerking off probably helps prevent pimples, as it relieves tensions, anxieties, and the kind of nervousness that makes kids pick at their faces.

Also, masturbating draws off those male hormones your fourteen-year-old body is overproducing and which are the main cause of pimples.

If God didn't want you to jerk off, he would have made your arms shorter.

Ask your dad. He'll tell you it never did him any harm.

When you jerk off, just try to do it as slowly as possible, so you won't have premature ejaculation problems later.

And, while you're doing it, be sure to think of girls. I mean, as opposed to hens or sheep.

The most important thing is: there is no such word as *alot*.

Love Never Faileth,
Mark Edwards

(March 26)

Dear Mark Edwards:

Recently we discovered our family doctor has put our 13-year-old daughter on contraceptive pills.

My husband wants to sue not only the doctor but the pharmacist who filled the prescription as well, but I'm not so sure.

A Concerned Mother

Dear Concerned Mother:

You might as well hang a red light outside your daughter's bedroom.

Before you start suing people, I suggest you sit down and have a quiet conversation with your family doctor.

Maybe he knows something you don't know.

Dear Mark Edwards:

Every morning I wake up with a headache, a dry mouth, and blood-shot eyes, and slightly sick to my stomach. The only thing I find that helps it is a bloody mary before lunch.

What's wrong with me?

Morning Miseries

Dear Morning Miseries:

Don't worry. You're not pregnant.

Dear Mark Edwards:

I'm 14 and I really like masturbating, but everybody says it will give me pimples. I don't have many pimples, but I don't want them. I want to masturbate.

Jerry Jerk-off

Dear Jerry Jerk-off:

Take lots of cold showers, develop a respectful relationship with a girl, and isn't there some other sport you could enjoy?

The usual advice is, you should go out and break your legs playing football.

Dont' sweat it, son. One or two other people in the history of the world have survived being 14.

Dear Mark Edwards:

Every time my husband comes near me, I begin to sneeze.

Could it be because I'm having sexual fantasies about the man who cuts our lawn?

Sneezy

Dear Sneezy:

Could be.

I suspect you've taken to sneezing in front of your husband because deep down you feel guilty about your fantasies about the lawn-service man. Therefore I suggest you tell your husband about your fantasies. Either that, or move north, where the lawn-cutting season is shorter.

March 27

Dear ME:

Last night, while we were reading in bed, Pamela threw the newspaper on the floor, uttered a theatrical sigh, allowed a dramatic pause while she studied her thumbnail, and said: "Do you mind my telling you that I hate your new column?"

"Yes."

"It's so cheap. It's sleazy."

"We can't all be filum critics."

"What caused you to let Jim talk you into such a stupid thing?"

"Two martinis and a beer."

"'Dear Mark Edwards, Dear Mark Edwards' all over the page. 'I'm a fourteen-year-old boy who likes to masturbate.' Disgusting!"

"It's where it's at, babe."

"It's not where it's at, Mark. These people are just spewing all over you."

"Sometimes I spew back."

"Heartfelt advice: 'Move north, where the lawn-cutting season is shorter.' Is that intelligent?"

"No, but it's funny."

"It's not."

"It is, goddamn it."

"Will you tell me one reason why you took on this stupid column?"

"It's better than working on the copy desk."

"It's not. At least there you had the dignity of true labor."

"'The dignity of true labor.' Bullshit. You want to know what's funny? That's funny."

"Why did you take on this column?"

"I get paid more. Now I'm earning almost as much as you pay in taxes."

"Who cares about that?"

"I care about that. The downtrodden masses always care. The treaders—seldom. The haves haven't to care; the have-nots have. How do you like that petunia?"

"All I can say is I'm glad I don't write my film column under your name. It's bad enough that one of us is being laughed at."

"Sorry to be an embarrassment to you."

She rolled onto her side—away from me—muttering, "I just never thought I'd be married to a lovelice column."

"I never thought I'd be married to someone who sees ten, twenty movies a week. Is that a grown-up thing to do?"

"Good night, dear Mark Edwards."

"Good night, Pamela Jensen."

Dear ME, I don't need to tell me that Pamela isn't exactly my first wife.

Is everything I do wrong?

Or is it the way in which I do everything that's wrong?

2.

Dear Mark Edwards:

Me and some of the other ladies would like you to print our letter, if you've got the balls.

We earn our livings by walking the streets—usually at night, but not always, you know, we're not ashamed of what we do, making a living, that's more than you can say for some people —we're called street walkers, you know, not *night* walkers, for Chrissake—meeting men, some of them are real important jacks, like judges, doctors, I had a state senator once—anyway, more important than most cops! givin' them a few minutes of pleasure, a little lovin' up, you know, what's wrong with that?

Why do these cops have to hassle us so much?

Every coupla nights the van comes down the street, the fuzz jump out, open the back doors, start yellin', "Everybody in, everybody in!" One night, Mark, they almost threw a couple of Roman Catholic nuns in the wagon with us. Boy, were they scared! They were just on the sidewalk. One of the cops finally said to one of the penguins (the cops thought the nuns were two of us dressed up in drag. Weird! Who'd think of that? Who would have guessed what turns on cops?), "Hey, aren't you Frankie Doyle's sister, the one that used to blow the trumpet at the Sacred Heart?" or something like that, and she goes, "Yes, yes I am" and still this cop stands there, hat back, ears flappin' in the breeze, hands on his hips, snappin' his chewin' gum, the rest of us in the wagon already, shoutin' at them to hurry up and get us down to the station so we can get back to work, and he says to the other cop, "Hey, Philly, want to bring 'em in anyway? Give Frankie a laugh."

I mean, that's the way they are, Mark—real wise guys. Not at all serious about their profession.

Well, we earn more at our profession, and are alot more serious about it, by and large, and they know that, Mark, and they resent it.

Every time they take us in each one of us looses a hundred, two hundred, maybe even three hundred bucks—especially if they stand on the sidewalk after they get us in the van flirting with a coupla penguins!

The fuzz aren't allowed to hassle anybody else in the execution of their making a living. Why us?

The Ladies
(Ms. Silva Mellon)

March 28

Dear Ladies:

I was a police beat reporter long enough to know that if the cops are hassling you too much, most likely it's for one of the following reasons:

1. You're rolling too many stiffs, ripping off too many wallets. Seems like it, if you say an hour's ride to the station can cost you as much as three hundred bucks in income. Remember, darlings, the public would rather have the clap than lose their credit cards. Don't kill the goose that lays the golden yum-yum, to use your coin.

2. Your pimpy baby isn't paying off enough at the station

house. Sometimes the standard fines and court costs fall below the cost of living indices, thus it's cheaper for your pimpy baby to run you through the courts than spread the bread at the station house. So the precinct bigwigs aren't any happier at this situation than you are. They hate to see their supplemental income—for which they've spent years keeping their noses clean, working their way up through the ranks—go to the courts. Give your pimpy baby a few lashes.

3. Or you're not giving the cops on the beat enough nookies of their own. Be kind to your neighborhood cop. They're human, too, you know. If they get it off screwing around with people dressed up like nuns, then dress up like nuns. Pray, what's the harm? If calling them "Father" doesn't work, try "Monsignor."

Love Never Faileth,
Mark Edwards

March 26

Dear Mr. Edwards:

I have never read a column like yours in my life, but entering my office this morning I heard and saw my nurse and receptionist-secretary giggling over your column, and so bought a copy of your newspaper and read your column while eating my luncheon. There had seemed something particularly significant, one might even say relevant, in the nature of their giggles.

I wish to express my gratitude, and, I daresay, the gratitude of many of my colleagues, as well as that of some pharmacists, if I may speak for them, for your advice to that hysterical woman who signed herself "A Concerned Mother" in this morning's column.

By all means, instead of rushing off and suing her family doctor and pharmacist and whomever else considered at blame for the state of the world as it is today, she and her irate husband first had better sit down for a quiet conversation with their family doctor, in accordance with your good advice.

Indeed their family doctor does know something they don't know.

When I began practicing family medicine thirty-two years ago, in this reasonably quiet, suburban town, I was confronted with an unwanted pregnancy about every month or five weeks. Except for perhaps an average of two patients a year who were mature, married women who simply could not or did not want to bear a child for one reason or another, the average age of these unwed mothers-to-be was about eighteen and a half, or nineteen.

In recent years, since the advent of the Pill, I have four or five patients with unwanted pregnancies coming to me a month.

The difference is between eleven or twelve a year then and about sixty a year now.

The suburban town in which I practice has not changed that much.

I did not study medicine to become an abortionist.

Of most significance is that the preponderance of these patients are fourteen and a half and fifteen years old!

Yes, young girls come to me with developing bodies which are already smooth and muscular. Thanks to public school sports programs, none of them have a hymen intact after kindergarten.

Their panties and bras (if they wear them) are usually far prettier and more expensive than the rotten jeans or corduroys and sweaters they wear as outer clothes. It does not require a man to be young to suspect that their inner clothes are far more for public display than their outer clothes.

In the area of their breasts, often they will have pasties of lovebirds or some such thing stuck to their skin.

In their crotches, I have seen pasties of alligators, snakes, elephants, anteaters, hands with indicative fingers extended—even minute signs with arrows which read "This way"!

I've asked what these things are for.

Invariably the answer is some variation of: "For close friends."

I prescribe the Pill for these idiotic children, now from the age of about eleven and a half on, instruct them thoroughly in their use, urge them to use them, without either asking or notifying their parents.

For boys of the same age, instead of handing out lollipops, I now toss them a pack of rubbers. (I have noticed it causes them to return to the office with minor complaints far more frequently.)

It is not that I am making a moral decision for these children. The decision has been made—by them, by their society, and by their parents.

Yet I, and I'm sure others, live in mortal fear of the situation described by your hysterical "Concerned Mother"—that some hypocritical parent will discover her child's contraceptives and institute malpractice proceedings without consulting with the family physician.

I have had enough parents in my office weeping, saying, "How could this happen without our suspecting a thing!"

Of course, abortion is taken no more seriously by some of these children than the monthly visit to the orthodontist to get their braces tightened. For others—those who still have their dolls tossed about their beds—it can be a traumatic experience.

Now, I ask you, what is a doctor to do?

Patient confidentiality extends even to children, at least as a practical matter. If I said to parents, in contemporary parlance, "It is clear to me your twelve-year-old is fucking around," shortly I would find my practice limited to the treatment of varicose veins, and, of more importance, hundreds of babies a year would be had in the Town Wood.

I regret the length of this letter, but many, if not all, of us family physicians are confronted constantly by this touchy matter, and do appreciate your giving it an airing.

In the style of the rest of your correspondents, I sign myself,

Dolittle, M.D.

(Dr. Harry Ewing)

March 30

Dear Dr. Ewing:

If your figures are correct, that you're getting five times the patients now with unwanted pregnancies than you did thirty years ago, I guess that must allay my suspicions that you're just a dirty old man getting your cheapies in the office with "young girls . . . with developing bodies which are already smooth and muscular" and alligator pasties in their crotches, fantasizing juvenile sexual activities like you never had.

Gee, I'm sorry for thinking such a thing.

So you didn't study medicine to be an abortionist?

Well, you built your own practice, Doc. It took you thirty-two years to develop a nice, warm practice for your old age, right?

My advice to you is to have your imagination removed by surgery, go back to handing out lollipops, and read up on the last thirty years' of advances regarding the treatment of varicose veins.

It's not my column your nurse and receptionist-secretary are laughing at.

It's the idea that you're long overdue for a malpractice suit!

Love Never Faileth,
Mark Edwards

March 30

Dear ME:

Somehow I'm getting to like the DEAR MARK EDWARDS column better, the more it annoys Pamela.

I had lunch with Jim Krikorian yesterday.

"The column's going pretty well," he said, after our pots of martini had been set before us.

"My wife doesn't like it."

Jim aimed his watery eyes at the fartherest corner of the ceiling. "How could she? Film critic for *Hawthorne's* magazine. . . ."

Would Mari like the column?

Would her violet eyes look up and smile at me as she read it?

"Filum."

"What?"

"Filum critic. It's traditional. Like pronouncing the names of fashion designers with a French accent, even if they're born and raised in Ohio."

I dream of Mari.

Pronounced Mar, *like the Sea, with the true sound of* E.

"Intellectual," Jim said. "Very intellectual."

"I'll say. She hasn't reviewed a movie about a boy and a dog in over a decade."

"Have they made a movie about a boy and a dog this decade?"

"They must have. Some of the filums must have made money. None she reviews ever has."

Jim gulped from his pot. "I remember when movies used to be about people."

"Movies are no longer about people." *No one would make a movie, a filum, of Mari and Mark. Pamela Jensen wouldn't like it.* "They're about how the cameraman got syphilis."

"I never read your wife's column," Jim said. "In fact, I never read *Hawthorne's*. I gave it up. They've gone years without an editorial idea."

"*Hawthorne's* isn't about people, either."

"I suspect she gets paid a lot. Writing a film column—excuse me, filum column—for a weekly national magazine."

"About two and a half times what I get—thanks to you and the publisher of our illustrious newspaper."

"That all?" Jim asked vacantly.

"Is that all?"

"Gee, that's not much. I'd think she'd be earning more than that."

"Thanks a heap."

"Together you have a pretty good salary."

"Together we have terrible expenses. Four children between us, all away at school. My alimony payments. Have you seen the crummy place we're living?"

"You've never invited me."

"Of course not. It looks like a locker room for car-wash employees. Why would we invite you?"

"How did you happen to marry Pamela, anyway?"

"I met Pamela at a World Premiere of a dreadful movie. I forget the name of it. I think its World Premiere was the only time it was shown on the screen. The movie's public relations man handed ducats around to us poor working stiffs on the copy desk, a sure sign they knew it was stinko. They were trying to paper the house. I should have known. I went. So I met Pamela."

"Sorry. I still don't see how M. Edwards, copy editor of our grungy metropolitan daily, breaks through a movie premiere crowd and marries the eminent, national filum critic Pamela Jensen."

"I was just divorced," I said.

"Go on."

"I hated everybody at the theater ignoring me."

"Yes?"

"I mean, me, Mark Edwards, who once won a United Press International Award for my coverage of an airport fire."

"That was twelve years ago," Jim said.

"Eleven."

"Fame is fleeting."

"Flame is fleeting?"

"Bet you can't say that again."

"Flame is feeting."

"Told you so."

"Mark Edwards," I said, more modestly, "lately of the copy desk."

"You hadn't had a by-line in five years."

"No."

"By the way, why not?"

"I was writing a book. Trying to write a book."

"About what?"

"About what?" I repeated, as if trying to remember.

"Just curious," Jim said. "About what?"

"Well . . ."

"About what?"

"Airport fires."

"Jerk. Trying to make a career out of one airport fire."

"One UPI Award, buddy. Not everyone wins a UPI Award."

"Almost everyone," Jim said. "How did the book turn out?"

"Great."

"I haven't noticed it in the windows of Brentano's, Dalton's, Doubleday's. . . ."

"Well . . ."

"Not a candidate for the Pulitzer?"

"It wasn't published."

"No!"

"The publishers thought it wouldn't sell well at the airports," I said, putting the blame squarely where it belonged.

"You spent five years of your life, five years of your career, five years on the copy desk, writing an unsellable book?"

"Well, it was a big fire, Jim. A big award."

"Wow," Jim said. "No wonder I outrank you. No wonder I'm your editor. I never tried to write a thing in my life."

"Can't blame me for trying," I said.

"Sure I can." Jim rolled the rest of his martini down his throat. "Easily. You screwed up. So this poor turd, Mark Edwards, copy editor, gets a free ducat from a flack papering the house for the World Premiere of a stinko movie, and deservedly feels ignored by all the swells in the theater lobby. How did you meet and marry La Eminent Jensen?"

"Somehow she seemed to be ignoring me more than anyone else."

"To ignore is not a relative term." Jim looked thirstily toward the waiter. "You cannot be ignored more by one person than by another. If you were ignored, you were totally ignored."

"Pamela's ignoring me bothered me more than anyone else's ignoring me."

"That's better."

"Thank you."

"So what did you do?"

"I went up to her."

"A karate chop to the neck to get her attention?"

"A little nudge on the front part of her left shoulder."

How had I gotten Mari's attention?

(How had I lost it?)

"You always were subtle, Mark."

"And I said, 'I think your filum criticism stinks.'"

At least I had Mari's attention, once, so long ago, for so short a time.

"And what did Pamela do? A knee raised quickly to your crotch?"

"She kissed me on the cheek and took me by the hand, and we went into the theater together."

"Ah! Love at first sight."

"Exactly."

"Is she a masochist?"

"Just a liberal."

"Same thing." Jim waved impatiently at the waiter for two more martinis. "So how do you explain Pamela Jensen's openness to you? She could have married a successful producer. A successful director. A successful actor. Why did she marry a copy-desk schlepper?"

Mari could have married anyone, too. Someone on the way somewhere, someone who thought in terms of today and tomorrow and tomorrow instead of today, just today, and baseball. She could have married anyone. I suppose she did.

"Pamela doesn't spell so well," I said. "Her spelling needs going over."

"That must be it," Jim said. "That must be it."

Over our second martinis, Jim got back to the point.

"Movies just aren't about people anymore," he said. "*Hawthorne's* magazine isn't about people."

No, the filum I had seen with Pamela that night hadn't been about people.

It hadn't been about Mari and Mark

It hadn't been about walking hand in hand with Mari through an urban spring, duffel coats and pizza stains, scuffed shoes on sticky sidewalks, violet eyes in a sea of skin delicious to the touch, passing, as we walked, passing barren branches against the sky, then passing budding leaves, soon, too soon, in the fullness, and, it seems, the completion of our love, of her love, passing trees heavy with green, passing June's sun stabbing at us from the corners of glass-walled buildings; shiny green panties, tassels from her tits, those obscene high-heeled shoes! a warm room which was our own; love upon a mattress on the floor. God, what time was it? we never knew what time it was upon that mattress on the floor in that warm room which was our own. It was twenty years ago—that's what time it was. Time that passed and became past.

Mari and Mark

As a film about people (Pamela's husband and his earlier friend), I know what Pamela's review would be: "Sentimental . . . contrived . . . not at all the way life is. . . ."

Well. It isn't the way life is.

Is it?

It's the way life was.

Or was it?

"Your column, Mark," Jim said. "That's about people."

"More than anybody ever wanted to know about them," I muttered.

"Get lots of mail?"

"Bags of it. The Post Office is thinking of giving me my own zip code."

"DEAR MARK EDWARDS. That's really about people. What they're really thinking about. What their problems really are."

I've noticed that on the second martini *the People* usually become *they*. It must be the ice.

(*And on the first martini, I seem to dream of Mari.*)

"Pretty soon," Jim said, "we must do a readership survey. See what the people are reading in the newspaper these days."

"You mean: to see if they're reading my new column."

"That—and other things."

"My readership will never beat the readership of the sports pages."

"Don't be too sure," Jim said.

"Nothing ever has."

"Amazing," said Jim Krikorian. "The popular interest there is in wrecked knee cartilage."

"Is that what makes the people read the sports pages?"

"What else?" Jim said. "That's mainly what the sports pages are about. Isn't it? Wrecked knee cartilage: now, that's human. . . ."

There followed an extended list of problems Jim Krikorian considers human—from wrecked knee cartilage to bow-legged-ness, crossed-eyedness, non-matching ears, baldness, corns, sinking gums—and lamp chops completely surrounded by peas.

March 27

Dear Mr. Edwards:

I have handed your letter of March 25, addressed to my wife, to my attorneys this morning, instructing them to institute whichever suits against you they deem appropriate.

Apparently my wife wrote you expressing a genuine concern regarding discovering contraceptive devices among the belongings of my thirteen-year-old daughter. However ill-advised her letter, it was written with sincerity.

Under no circumstances does she deserve such a vituperative attack as set forth in your personal letter to her.

You suggested she is fat; she is plump.

You suggested she drinks too much; she drinks no more than I.

You suggested she indulges in sexual fantasies through our adolescent daughter; I have never contemplated a more obscene conjecture.

You'll be hearing from my attorneys.

Donald Bainbridge

March 30

Dear Mr. Bainbridge:

You're suing your family doctor, your neighborhood pharmacist, and now your friendly local reporter.

Next I suppose you'll bring charges of treason against your mailman for delivering this letter to you.

Why don't you learn to duel with wet tea bags?

Love Never Faileth,
Mark Edwards

(April 1)

Dear Mark Edwards:

I have never read a column like yours in my life, but on behalf of myself and my colleagues, I wish to express the most profound gratitude to you for your advice to the "Concerned Mother" who discovered contraceptive pills among the belongings of her 13-year-old daughter.

Thirty-two years ago, when I began practicing family medicine, an average of 11 or 12 patients with unwanted pregnancies came to me a year—and their average age was 18 or 19.

In recent years, an average of 60 patients suffering unwanted pregnancies have come to me a year—the preponderance of them 14 and 15 years old!

Indeed, as you so wisely write, the family doctor does know something you don't know!

In prescribing contraceptives for these youngsters, I am not making a moral decision for them. The moral decision has already been made —by them, their society, and their parents.

What else is a doctor to do?

Dr. Dolittle

Dear Dr. Dolittle:

Thanks for taking the time to write, Doc.

Dear Mark Edwards:

I was born with, well, I guess my ears don't match. I mean, each other. One is smaller and points up to the sky.

The bigger one—and it is bigger—hangs down like a half-filled knapsack.

It was all right when I was a little kid, but now the girls are noticing it.

Wearing long hair doesn't do any good. One side the hair bulges out like a pillow. And on the other side the ear peeks out like Mount Everest above the clouds.

Flop-Flip

Dear Flop-Flip:

A plastic surgeon can balance your ears faster than you can balance your bike tires.

Consult your family doctor—and while there, see if he's still handing out lollipops.

Ten or 12 years running a newspaper route should take care of the hospital bill.

If you don't want to do that, look on the bright side.

When you die, you can leave your ears to two different people.

Dear Mark Edwards:

Me and some other ladies earn our livings walking the streets, giving a little pleasure to men, you know, but all the cops do is hassle us, hassle us, hassle us.

Cops aren't allowed to hassle other people so much engaged in the pursuit of their livings.

Why us?

The Ladies

Dear Ladies:

Society is changing its point of view on many issues these days. Why shouldn't Society change its view regarding the world's oldest profession?

In some areas, the ladies are forming Intimate Entertainment Unions. Some are even going so far as to hire Public Relations Representatives.

Don't forget your Motto, ladies: You Can Try Anything Once.

April 2

Dear Dad:

Everything's going fine here at school, except Algebra, I mean, like how many years do I have to take this shit?

I mean, like who cares what X equals or N equals? They're just shitty little letters getting back at us 'cause they're not closer to the front of the alphabet, right?

Hey, look, the biggie against St. Axelrood's happens May 20

and my roommate, Tony, plays second base, and I know what kind of a maniac you are about baseball (you would have been a great sportswriter if UPI hadn't weirded you up by giving you that award for covering that airport fire when I was four years old, right?) and we were sort of wondering if you might like to drive out and see the game? We can fox a bottle of bourbon somewhere.

And, hey, say thanks to that woman you're living with for sending me that box of sanitary napkins. Tell her I still need 'em.

Yours, for chrissake,
Shelley

3.

Dear Shelley:

Thanks for your invitation to your school's "biggie" baseball game. I hadn't realized Rounds School had fielded an all-girls baseball team. My, how things change. Tell your roommate, Antoinette, I'll do my best to be there.

No letter from me could be complete without corrections.

First, please do not refer to your stepmother as *that woman I live with*. She loves you very much. Besides, her income being considerably greater than mine, it is she who is paying most of your tuition.

Second, X and N are not *shitty little letters*. Remember, please, I use letters to earn my living—all of them—and thus am able to contribute to your support at that expensive boarding school. Admittedly, the letter X, by and of itself, has not provided all that much income over the years, but where would *except* be without it? E'cept? Fi'ation? No'ious? The dear little letter N has been pulling its weight nobly all these years, despite its humble place in the nalphabet.

The new column is going well.

Your father

April 3

Dear Mark Edwards:
My breasts are too small. Anything I can do about it?

Teensy Titsy
(Sally Jeffries)

April 5

Dear Sally:
Too small for what?

Love Never Faileth,
Mark Edwards

April 3

Dear Mark Edwards:
Everybody thinks all women are demure little powder puffs who want to be treated like Queen Victoria.

Well, some of us are, and some of us aren't!

Every once in a while I want a little rough-and-tumble, you know, Mark? *Violence!*

Now, my husband's the nicest man in the world. He wouldn't hurt a flea. The fruitcake.

I scream at him and yell at him and call him a pansy and all he does is shrivel up.

I slap at him and hit him and punch him and all he does is put my arms at my side and make love in Standard Position Number One.

He doesn't even bite me!

Over the years, I've accumulated some pretty good equipage —a few wide leather belts, one of those tassely whips with one of those braided butts that look like a dear, sweet penis—for him, you see—a soft leather codpiece, thigh-high boots, biceps bands—even one of those stiff leather headband things that come down in a triangle between his eyes. I've bought all these things myself, Mark, saving a little from each week's food budget.

I figure if I can ever raise him to show any kind of violence, Mark, I can show him what I've got!

But no! All I ever get is soft, gentle love! love! love!

How do I make a man out of this twerp?

Suffering Lady
(Lucy Dodson)

April 5

Dear Mrs. Dodson:

Indeed, you do have a different idea of manliness from that held by many of your gender.

I suggest you take your husband aside some quiet evening and show him your equipage—your wide leather belts, your tassely whip with the braided butt that looks like a dear, sweet penis, your soft leather codpiece, thigh-high boots, biceps bands, and eyes-separator.

If that doesn't make him violent, nothing will.

Love Never Faileth,
Mark Edwards

April 4

Dear Mark Edwards:

I'm doing six to ten for a mugging incident I had nothing to do with.

They all said I used a knife, a big knife, nine inches long, a deadly weapon, even showed it in court, I'd never seen it before, well, that cooked my goose, you can bet, it fried my ass, all right.

I never used a knife with a blade more than two and a half, three inches long.

There's a big difference between a deadly weapon and a face-slasher.

And I can't get anybody to listen!

Fried Ass
(Jumbo Dondershine)

April 7

Dear Mr. Dondershine:

As far as I'm concerned, you're a filthy punk and deserve everything you get, and more.

Six to ten for mugging someone at knife point? They should have thrown you into a dungeon and melted down the key.

Don't write me again, punk.

> Love Never Faileth,
> Mark Edwards

April 7

Dear Dad:

I read Tony your letter referring to him as Antoinette and he laughed so hard he cracked his elbow on the floor rolling off the bed.

Your darling Rounds School has been coed for years now, Dear Daddy Dodderer.

Which reminds me of something I've been meaning to mention for many moons now.

Can't you parent-types do something about these beds here at school? I know you Eminent Adults consider us fifteen-year-olds half-formed little animals, but when was the last time you tried it in a single bed? Jesus, it gets hot.

Hope you can make the game, baseball freak. Will that woman you live with be coming with you? Got a nice letter from Military Markey, the Curious Cadet. Oh, and hey, listen— any chance of your smuggling some coke over the state border for us?

> Your daughter,
> Shelley

April 1

Dear Mark Edwards:

I observe in your column, in this morning's newspaper, a letter signed "The Ladies" from persons who clearly are not ladies.

Not only that but, doubtlessly from your sense of courtesy, however misguided, in your answer you addressed them as "Ladies."

They are whores.

In my world, the term "lady" continues to mean something, and definitely not the thing these persons apparently represent.

A Lady
(Mrs. Philip Horgan)

April 7

Dear Mrs. Horgan:

Don't tell me you want me to break out the word "whore" again.

Love Never Faileth,
Mark Edwards

April 3

Dear Mark Edwards:

Bad enough the tawdry cunts signed themselves "ladies"—do you have to address them back that way?

We're not ladies, you shiny-assed bastard.

We're women.

And you better believe it.

Up yours.

Jo Blow
(Ms. Jo Blow)

April 7

Dear Ms. Blow:

But would you have me address them as "tawdry cunts"?

Love Never Faileth,
Mark Edwards

April 9

Dear ME:

I received a letter from Shelley and hit the roof to such an extent that I did something I never do, swore I'd never do.

I called her mother.

"What do you want?" she said, as if it were a few moments ago I had last bothered her.

"Merriam, I've just received a letter from Shelley."

"She writes you?"

"Yes, she writes me. I'm her father."

"You'd never know it."

"Well, she knows it, and I know it, and that's all that matters."

"I know it, too," said Merriam.

"Merriam, are we going to have a polite, civil conversation or not? Answer me that. That's all I want to know."

"I don't know," she answered. "Let's see how it goes."

"Look, Merriam, her letter says her roommate is a boy."

"Not really," sighed Merriam. "Officially Gandy Cummings is still her roommate."

"Then where is she? What happened to her? Where's good old Candy?"

"Gandy. Her name is Gandy. Have you met her?"

"No. I don't think so. How do I know?"

"Then why do you call her 'good old Gandy'?"

"At least I know she's not a he."

"Really, Mark."

"Listen, I get paid for being funny. Laugh a little."

"A very little."

"I only get paid a little," I said, remembering I was speaking to my ex-wife, whose lawyers doubtlessly were looking for any indication of an improvement in my income. "What happened to this Gandy person?"

"Bobby? Donny?"

"What's a Bobby-Donny?"

"A Bobby-Donny is what happened to Gandy. She moved into his room. Officially, she's still Shelley's roommate, but she lives in Bobby-Donny-whatever's room."

"I see. And was this Tony-whoever, here in Shelley's letter, he was Bobby-Donny's roommate and therefore he got thrown out and simply moved in with Shelley?"

"No," Merriam said slowly. "It's more complicated than that. Haven't you visited the school lately?"

"That's not important. How does this Tony character come to be sleeping with my fifteen-year-old daughter?"

"You still call it 'sleeping,' Mark. You should be paid more for being funny."

"I'm not being funny! There is nothing funny in this situation, Merriam."

"Just in your reaction to it."

"I'm not reacting! I'm asking a question. A Tony is sleeping with my daughter, and you knew about it!"

"Of course I know about it."

"And you've done nothing about it?"

"Of course I haven't done anything about it. What makes you think Shelley should have a room all to herself?"

"Merriam!"

"She's not a Queen Bee."

"Well, it rather sounds like she is a Queen Bee!"

"Stop shouting, Mark. I'm getting an echo."

"Listen, Merriam," I said, very calmly. "You're not explaining very well how you could know some boy is sleeping with our fifteen-year-old daughter at school, and—and—and you've done nothing about it."

"What's to explain? Basically, it's very simple."

"You said it was complicated."

"Basically, it's simple. Let me put it this way, Mark. If you had to share a room with somebody, whom would you rather share it with—a boy or a girl?"

"Merriam—"

"Do you expect it to be any different at age fifteen?"

"Merriam—"

"It's more interesting sharing a room with someone of the opposite sex. Also, it's more fun."

"Merriam—"

"Girls and boys complement each other, Mark, anatomically. You've noticed that, I think?"

"Merriam!"

"Usually, at least by the age of fifteen almost everybody has noticed that girls and boys complement each other anatomically. I'm not absolutely sure of this, Mark, but I suspect that structurally a girl's body and a boy's body fit more neatly into a bed together, more comfortably, you know, probably leaves more room, than two girls' bodies or two boys' bodies in any one bed."

"But why do they all have to be in one bed!" I shouted.

"Why, Mark," she answered. "To fuck."

That, Dear ME, is how much Merriam has changed!

When we were first married she thought my wanting to use Vaseline some kind of a perversion.

"Merriam . . ."

"To continue . . ." She cleared her throat. (Why I married a college lecturer in Astronomy I don't know. A college lecturer in Astronomy and then a philgm critic! Anything to support my natural sense of inferiority, I suppose. The very first girl I was in love with—*not Mari*—played the violin and laughed at my oboe.) Merriam tested her cleared throat: "To continue?"

"Yes, Merriam darling."

"You have to admit that boys and girls living together is for the social good."

"I do?"

"You do."

"I don't."

"Take you and me, for example."

"No."

"You and I could fuck all right together—"

"Whaddaya mean 'all right'? Listen, sister—"

"Make babies and all that—after all, Mark, we did make two of them—but the thing we had never learned was how to live together. Think about that a moment."

I thought about it.

"Get my point, Mark, darling?"

"You're going to bring up my clipping my toenails in bed again, Merriam, and leaving them on the sheets—"

"No, I wasn't, darling. You have far more disgusting habits I could resort to in any conversation."

"Disgusting? What disgusting?"

"Inconsiderate. If these children are learning to live with each other, with consideration for each other as people and individuals, then perhaps they'll have more satisfactory relations with each other than you and I ever did or, we could say, do have."

"Jesus."

"If, however, you are publicly advocating masturbation, as you did in your column the other day—"

"What!"

"Oh, I'm sorry, darling. Didn't I read something about cold showers and a respectful relationship with a girl?"

"I am not advocating masturbation."

"Darling, at least you must admit you referred to masturbation as a *sport*. A sport, darling, is something usually played in company, with one or more others, and, almost invariably, competitively. Only a very odd person indeed could refer to masturbation as a *sport*."

"Merriam, you are the meanest, stupidest bitch I ever—"

"Oh, by the way, darling, how's Pamela?"

"She's wunnerful," I said, softly. "Wunnerful."

"Tell her I read her all the time. Her punctuation has improved since she took you on."

"Merriam, I'm going to call the school and have a reasonable discussion with whoever's in charge out there on this matter."

"I wouldn't, darling."

"Apparently you haven't."

"Shelley would never forgive you."

"I will be perfectly reasonable—"

"Suggest cold showers and sports programs? Saltpeter in the scrambled eggs? By the way, have you heard from Markey lately?"

"No."

"Neither have I. I do wish you hadn't insisted on sending him to that military school."

"Merriam, I get paid for giving people my advice."

"Mark, no one ever got football knees making love. Ta-ta, darling. I consider we've had a polite, civil conversation—under the circumstances."

I knew I shouldn't have called her.

I should have just called the school.

What, am I crazy, looking for moral support from an ex-wife? Even if she is Shelley's mother?

Well, she's not the Shelley's mother I knew.

The Shelley's mother I knew wouldn't make love with the record player on. She said she hated the idea Barbra Streisand was watching her.

Instead of calming me down, she got me madder.

So I sat down to have some bourbon before calling the school. What's this world coming to?

It's all the smut they read.

THEY. THE PEOPLE.

When I finally called the school (I don't know to whom I spoke) I got very little satisfaction.

I asked them what the hell they thought they were running out there, a boarding school or a French farce.

I told them that if I wanted my daughter to live that way, I know somebody who can get her three hundred dollars an hour, less court fines. She could pay her own tuition.

(I hope Shelley forgives me.)

(April 10)

Dear Mark Edwards:

My breasts are too small. Anything I can do about it?

Teensy

Dear Teensy:

On your behalf, I have consulted with the leading medical experts on the size of breasts.

Their best advice is that, if there is a body of water near you, such as a river or a lake, you take up rowing a boat as a sport.

They guarantee it will make you row-bust.

Dear Mark Edwards:

I'm in prison, doing a sentence from six to ten years, for mugging someone with a deadly weapon, a nine-inch knife, when I never used anything more than a face-slasher in my life.

I can't get anybody to listen to me!

Face-Slasher

Dear Face-Slasher:

No sympathy here, punk.

Anyone who assaults anybody with anything, anytime, ought to be imprisoned and the key thrown away.

Dear Mark Edwards:

Those prostitutes who wrote you are clearly not "ladies" as the term is used in my world.

Why did you address them as such?

A Lady

Dear Mark Edwards:
We prostitutes are not ladies—we're women, dammit.

Ms. Jo

Dear Girls:
I'm not the one having an identity crisis—you are.
Funk & Wagnalls dictionary defines "lady" as "a woman of good breeding or family; a gentlewoman."
I define "lady" as a person of the female gender who never, ever eats baked beans the same day she drinks bourbon.

Dear Mark Edwards:
Everybody thinks all women are demure little powder puffs who want to be treated like Queen Victoria.
Well, some of us are, and some of us aren't!
Every once in a while I want a little rough-and-tumble in our sex life, but how do I get this across to my husband?

Suffering Lady

Dear Suffering Lady:
I see you never eat baked beans the same day you drink bourbon.
My best suggestion is you discuss your desires peacefully with your playmate.
If he doesn't understand, get another playmate.

Dear Mark Edwards:
I'm a 15-year-old girl in a coed boarding school, and although the school went coed some years ago the dumb authorities still have two single beds in one room.
It's not realistic.
What can we do to make the dumb authorities provide double beds?

Shall We?

Dear Shall We?:
I suggest you take the matter up with your Student Council.
Of course, if Society—in this case, your School Authorities—condoned you half-formed little animals mucking around with each other, they'd provide the proper facilities.

4.

Dear ME:

Jim Krikorian called while I was hammering out the column.

"Guess who's got the biggest readership in the paper?"

"Buzz Hodd?"

"Who's he?"

"Your sportswriter, Jim. Your star sportswriter."

"Oh, yeah. The big fella."

"The one whose knees keep bumping against his lower belly when he walks."

"No, no. Not Hodd. You. DEAR MARK EDWARDS. You have the biggest readership in the paper. We just took a survey."

(People actually read this shit? I'd better get serious!)

"Of course," I said. "What did you expect?"

"How does that make you feel?"

"Like a fat person in an E-string rising through the top of a birthday cake."

"You feel unworthy, eh?"

"I didn't say that, exactly."

"Jeez, Mark. Love the way you keep the column issue-oriented. Sex for children. Whether prostitutes are ladies. Love it."

"It's not disgusting?"

"Disgusting? Mouse spoor in vanilla ice cream! It's where it's at, baby. Are those letters for real?"

"Realer than you'll ever know."

"How about that kid with the flip-flop ears? You said when he dies he can leave his ears to two different people."

"I made that one up."

"I thought so."

"For you. It came from that lunch we had together. I thought it was funny."

"Funny, funny."

"I get a lot of letters like that, though. My breasts are two small, my nose is too big, my bed at boarding school is too small to fuck around in. . . ."

"But you make some of them up, right?"

"I make some of them up. Very few."

"Whatever you're doing, Mark—keep it up. Keep it issue-oriented, you know what I mean?"

"Yeah."

"Issue-oriented. Say, Mark. What would you think of trying for syndication?"

My hand tightened on the phone. "Syndication?"

That would mean an actual living income. Take-home pay that would actually make it to the front door. FAME! Appear in more newspapers than just one. Maybe many newspapers! Reach the fartherest corners of Pamela's national readership!

"Aw, gee, I dunno, Jim."

"The machinery for syndication is here. Might as well use it."

"Aw, gee, I dunno, Jim."

"Listen. In a matter of weeks your column has gotten the highest readership in the newspaper."

"Yeah . . ."

"Put together a dozen columns. Just the tear sheets, you know? Give 'em to me."

"Gee, I dunno, Jim."

"Listen, Mark. This stuff is national. International. 'Most every-body is afflicted with one sex or another. It's where people are at. Why not? We can try."

"Well. All right."

"Let me have 'em this afternoon. Give me the ones you feel are most issue-oriented."

Sugar plum fairies dance in my head.

April 11

Dear Mr. Edwards:

Parishioners have brought to my attention the column which runs in the daily newspaper under your salutation, DEAR MARK EDWARDS.

I wonder if you have any idea of the evil you are foisting upon the world?

Experiencing premarital and extramarital sexual relations is a sin, punishable by our Divine Father.

The sexual experience is to happen solely between husband and wife, lawfully married, and solely for the purpose of procreation.

Even within the marital bed, indulging in sexual activity with passion as the sole purpose of such activity is sinful perversion.

By discussing in your column such matters as supplying un-married children with contraceptives, prostitution, and violent sexual "play" you are granting such sinful matters a wider social acceptance; in God's truth, you are condoning them.

Now, I know how you and your ilk will respond: that these are real matters and you are treating them "realistically": I'm sure you can show me statistics and surveys and behavioral studies indicating the extent to which human beings give in to their baser instincts.

I, sir, can show you the Word of God, which is eternal, and which eternally condemns any false prophet, such as yourself.

Father William Lynd

April 14

Dear Father Lynd:

Judas Priest, you still believe that shit?

Bite your tongue!

Jesus, Buddy, when you add up all the centuries of sin committed in the name of God—mayhem, torture, murder, slavery, slaughter, genocide, starvation, deprivation, injustice, oppression, suppression, avarice, lies, theft—and you still have the motherfucking balls to preach that it's a Big Sin for a couple of warm naked bodies to get together and enjoy themselves however they can, then you're the biggest, stupidest, most hypocritical, deluded cunt of them all!

If you were born without balls, then you have my sympathy.

If you've spent your life squeezing your balls so tight they've shriveled, cracked, and turned to dust under the pressure of your own hands, then I pray God you live long enough in your misery to see the error of your ways.

Love Never Faileth,
Mark Edwards

April 12

TO: Mark Edwards
FROM: Monroe Lipton, Publisher

Dear Mark:

As you know, it's a matter of tradition, in this newspaper, for the Board of Directors and I to try to keep our hands off editorial affairs and restrict our activities to the business side of publishing—to try to earn enough from advertising to keep up with the ever-increasing cost of newsprint.

We consider that Jim Krikorian, the Managing Editor, should be able to run the editorial affairs of this newspaper without our interference.

For example, we have not yet told Jim about alot of the reaction to your column we've had over here on the business side of the building.

So far, a furniture store, which has been advertising through our newspaper for years, has dropped its advertising in protest of your column. A major department store—one of our biggest advertisers—has dropped some of its advertising, with a letter to me explaining that your column is the reason why. A similar situation has developed with a car dealership, except that the explanation was given over lunch.

Of course, Jim Krikorian does the hiring and firing on your side of the building.

I've gone through some of your columns myself. I must say I'm appalled to see the word "masturbate" in a family newspaper. I'm shocked out of my skin to read anyone writing for this newspaper advise anyone, such as "Suffering Lady," to have extramarital relations.

Our Founder, Governor Stapleton, must be whirling in his grave.

A word to the wise is sufficient, Mark.

April 14

TO: Monroe Lipton, Publisher
FROM: Mark Edwards
A word to the wise is sufficient.

April 13

Dear Mark Edwards:

This girl and I, we were going to have a baby.

I told her it was okay. I loved her. I just told her it would take me a few days to get things worked out. I even got a guy to give me an after-school job at his gas station and pay me in cash even before I got a Social Security card.

Well, she went to stay with her aunt, who's only a couple of years older than she is, and they took it out with a coat hanger.

Now I hate her.

What's bad is she's still bleeding.

Now I don't feel like doing anything about it, you know?

Bad Thom
(Thom. Mirto)

April 14

Dear Thom:

Get her to a doctor—FAST!

I would have called you, but I couldn't find any listing under "Mirto" in your town.

Look, kid, the girl probably thought she was doing you some

kind of favor. She probably did it this way out of some weirdo idea of love for you.

This is a medical problem. It may be a medical emergency.

Get to her parents, get to your parents (even though they've been treating you like a kid all your life—because you've been one—they weren't born yesterday), get her to any doctor you know, but DO IT NOW!

The idiot you should hate is her aunt.

> Love Never Faileth,
> Mark Edwards

April 13

Dear Mark Edwards:

All the girls in my high school carry contraceptive pills.

I've had my pack (with three missing) for years.

(I gave those three to the dog—who's an It.)

It's a status symbol, you know?

Don't believe everything you read.

> Ring-a-ding
> (Mina Knoedler)

April 15

Dear Mina:

You call carrying contraceptive pills around in your pocket a status symbol.

I call it an advertisement.

Pretty soon, somebody's going to ring your ding.

I sure hope more than three of your pills will be missing from your pack at that time.

> Love Never Faileth,
> Mark Edwards

April 15

Dear Shelley:

A friend told me the other day that he made an ill-considered, irate phone call to the administrators of his kid's school. Do you ever hear of such calls being made to your school?

My warmest regards to Tony. Assure him I will never refer to him as Antoinette again. I'd hate to have the dear boy's elbow permanently impaired.

Daddy Dodderer,
A Parent-Type

P.S. Of course I'll sneak Coke across the state border to you. Is it more expensive there? Wouldn't you rather have a case of fruit juice?

(April 16)

Dear Mark Edwards:

In reference to your recent columns, I am obliged to write and say that experiencing premarital and extramarital sexual relations is a sin, punishable by our Divine Father.

The sexual experience is to happen solely between husband and wife, lawfully married, and solely for the purpose of procreation.

Even within the marital bed, indulging in sexual activity with passion as the sole purpose of such activity is sinful perversion.

Father William Lynd

Dear Father Lynd:

Thanks for taking the time to write, Father.

Dear Mark Edwards:

In high school our daughter was doing the weekend pot-beer-wine thing and she didn't seem at all affected by it at first, and my wife and I decided it was just a necesary adjunct to American teen-aged social life.

She's 20 now, Mark, and has dropped out of nurses' training and has been using cocaine, we're pretty sure, and lately, we suspect, has begun on heroin.

It's killing us, seeing this kid's life being eaten away with drugs.

Mr. Morose

Dear Mr. Morose:

If it's any consolation to you, I receive a great many letters such as yours, reporting that a dear one is hooked on drugs.

The problem has become so common that there are resources available to those seeking advice or help in every community.

Probably the person you should approach first in seeking advice is your minister, rabbi, or priest.

Believe me, such professionals are well aware of these problems, have great understanding of them, and have experience and training in how to deal with these problems and how to advise you and your daughter realistically.

Dear Mark Edwards:
All the girls in my high school carry contraceptive pills.
I've had my pack (with three missing; I gave those three to my dog—who's an It) for years.
It's a status symbol, you know?
Don't believe everything you read.

Ring-a-Ding

Dear Ring-a-Ding:
I can't think of any better status symbols for teen-agers than the following:
1) Cleanliness and Consideration;
2) Doing as well in school as possible;
3) Playing sports vigorously and fairly.

Dear Mark Edwards:
This girl and I made a mistake and were going to have a baby.
I told her everything was all right, it would take time to work out, and I got an after-school job.
She went to visit an aunt, who is not much older than she is, and together they performed a primitive abortion.
Now I'm not sure how well my girl friend is. She may be sick.
I didn't want her to do this thing, and I don't know what to do about it.

Bad Thom

Dear Bad Thom:
Get to her parents, get to your parents, trust them (they've been treating you like a kid all your life because you've been one; realize they weren't born yesterday), but get proper medical attention for your girl friend as quickly as you can.

April 16

TO: James Krikorian, Managing Editor
FROM: Mark Edwards

As per your request, enclosed are a dozen tear sheets of the DEAR MARK EDWARDS column, to submit for possible syndication.

Sorry putting them together took longer than I thought, but, as per your advice, I tried to pick the most issue-oriented of the columns to date.

Also, Jim, sorry about today's dead-ass, deadly dull column, advising everybody to talk to their ministers, doctors, and parents, but I've been getting some flack from business-side, which, per usual, is seven leagues behind the real world.

I'll goose the column up again as soon as we get a smile from the front office.

April 16

TO: Monroe Lipton, Publisher
FROM: Mark Edwards

Enclosed tear sheet of today's column is to indicate to you and the other members of the Board of Directors how sufficient a word to the wise—in this case—is.

5.

Dear Mark Edwards:

I wrote you before, signing myself as "Suffering Lady"—about rough-and-tumble sex play?—and I just want to tell you how nice you were to write me personally and what a great man you are.

I did just as you said.

You solved all my problems for me!

Last night, after my husband came home and we'd had supper, I led him by the hand gently into the bedroom and slowly took off all his clothes.

He began to kiss me gently, I guess thinking we were just going to make love, and he got erect enough, and I kissed that, and while I was on my knees, I opened the bottom drawer of my bureau, just enough so I could get things out but he couldn't see inside (except maybe the sheen of the leather, and maybe get a whiff of the leather smell), and I took out the codpiece and, coming back to him, I lifted each of his feet by the ankle, making him step into it, and then lifted it slowly up his legs, finally bending his penis down into it.

Then, still kneeling before him, I kissed his penis through the soft leather codpiece, and then I bit the arch of it and pulled my head back, with it in my mouth, making my neck muscles show as if I was pulling that hard. His face, Mark, had turned this gorgeous, healthy apple pink, and there was this whole new look in his eyes!

I sat him on the edge of the bed and undressed in front of him, quickly, not too quickly, while these new, curious eyes of his watched, saying nothing, every once in a while looking down at himself in his codpiece.

Then I took out of the drawer the soft, leather thigh-high boots, and sitting on my haunches in front of him, I put them on his feet and ran them up his legs, looking all the time into his tight stomach muscles.

I bit him again, really making him feel it.

Then I took from the drawer one of his biceps bands, slipped that up his arm until it was tight against his muscle, and while he was looking at it, flexing his muscle beneath it, I put on him, like a crown, his headband, the triangle coming down between his eyes.

Getting the whip from the drawer, I looked back at him. He was crossing his eyes, looking up at the inside of the triangle.

Before he focused on me I had pressed the butt of the whip into the palm of his hand, closing his fingers over it, squeezing them, trying to hurt a little.

He looked from me to it to me again, his eyes wide and amazed!

I knelt before him again and bit him through the soft leather codpiece and this time pulled back hard!

He slapped the side of my head (he had to), knocking me sideways onto the floor, and he jumped up.

And there he stood over me, wary, whip in his hand, his whole body this gorgeous, apple pink, shining a little, with sweat, every muscle in his body tight, the arch of his penis in the codpiece standing out a mile.

And, boy, did he give it to me!

It was marvelous!

Heavenly!

Mark, we didn't get done playing until almost midnight!

And, then, when he was all undressed again, and we were in the bathtub, little flecks of blood in the bath water, we were equals again.

And this morning (at 10:15!) he called from the office to ask if we could do it again tonight!

Oh, Mark, I feel marvelous!

I thank you alot!

Any chance of your printing this letter in full?

> (No Longer) Suffering Lady
> (Lucy Dodson)

April 18

Dear Mrs. Dodson:

Tut, tut: think nothing of it.

I'm delighted you and your husband have found marital bliss.

The important thing, however, is that there is no such word as *alot*.

Somehow, I suspect your letter is a little too long for inclusion, but I will try to spread the joy of your experience however I can.

> Love Never Faileth,
> Mark Edwards

April 18

Dear ME:

So here I am, like an expired atheist in a funeral parlor: all dressed up with nowhere to go.

When I arrived home from the office shortly after six, Pamela was just getting out of the shower. The bathroom door opened and she entered the bedroom in a billow of steam, her hair done up.

Her evening clothes were laid out on our bed.

"Hmmmm," I said, kissing her. "I always did like you naked and soaking wet."

"Hmmmmm," she said. "Please confine your fantasies to your newspaper column."

"Why are they fantasies?"

"Because I've just had a shower," she said, "and there doesn't seem to be much hot water."

"Practical." I nodded. "Practical."

All the hot water had been converted to steam.

She sat at the dressing table to beat up her hair and make peace with her face.

"You should read a letter I got today." I sat on the edge of the bed. "Fantastic. I should have brought it home to you."

"All your letters are fantastic."

"This one was really fantastic." I pulled off my tie. "Although, I suppose, really not."

"Somehow," she said, while aerating her hair, "you have discovered a mine of human kookiness a thousand miles long and a thousand miles wide, which, from your own vanity and greed, you seem to have no compunction about bringing to the surface, to devastate the landscape."

"Ha!" I said, counting the number of neat phrases she had managed to get in among twelve licks of her hairbrush.

She turned and gave me her Pamela Jensen smile.

"What you're doing may be termed 'strip mining.' "

"Funny!" I said, sarcastically, wondering how I could use the line myself later. "Funny!"

I took off my jacket and put my back on the bed, leaving my feet on the floor.

"Anyway," I continued, "this woman wrote me this mammoth long letter, describing in most erotic detail her hours of sexual play with her husband the night before, during which she converted him from a gentle, loving man to the Marquis de Sade. Boots, leather codpiece, biceps bands, whips: the whole bit."

"Charming."

"She even described their sitting in a bathtub together, later, and the flecks of blood in the bath water. And she really used the word 'flecks.' 'Flecks of blood,' she wrote."

"How exciting."

"Actually, it was." Once, skiing in Vermont, Pamela actually had refused to make love in the snow. And it was March! "The public's ability to write well—when they're interested in what they're writing about—is most impressive."

"Most impressive." Pamela didn't agree.

"The funny thing is," I said, sitting up, "that this dame wrote the letter to me to thank me—for planning all this for her! For causing her sexual fulfillment! For saving her marriage!"

I was taking off my shirt.

"Had she written you before?"

"Yes."

"Had you answered her?"

"Yes. I always answer letters—if I can make any sense out of them at all."

"What did you say to her?"

"I don't remember."

I rolled my shirt into a ball, dried my armpits with it, and threw it into a corner.

Her eyes caught me in the dressing table mirror.

"Cinéma vérité," I said.

Going into the bathroom, I said, "By the way, Shelley tells me you send her sanitary napkins periodically. I didn't know that. Damned nice of you."

"It's my way," Pamela said, sucking stray lipstick off a tooth, "of my calling your fifteen-year-old daughter a bloody little cunt."

"What?"

"Which she is."

"Pamela!"

"Sometimes, Mark, the subtlety of my humor goes over your head."

"Hey!"

"Your daughter, Mark, is a wise-ass, with the morals of a mongoose and the intellectual potential of a sleeping rattlesnake."

The morals of a mongoose? That's what she said. How would she know what the morals of a mongoose are?

"Pamela, that's not fair. She's just a fifteen-year-old kid. She loves you very much."

"Like hell she does."

"She's even invited you out to their big baseball game next month. Her friend plays second base."

"She knows I hate baseball. Baseball needs the attentions of a good editor."

First she steps on Shelley, then she steps on baseball! while never once missing her stride at the dressing table.

Baseball needs the attentions of a good editor.

Not a bad line, though.

I went into the bathroom and wiped the steam off the mirror and looked into it.

I was still there. I mean, in the mirror. Somewhat.

While I was shaving, she said, "Have you heard from your son, Markey?"

"No. I haven't heard from Markey."

"You might try writing yourself."

"Thanks for your advice." Frankly, it had never occurred to me. I *answer* letters; I don't *write* them.

I said, "What thoughtful presents are you sending a thirteen-year-old boy in military school? Erotic pictures? Pornography?"

She said, "I've sent him a few of your columns."

Ooo.

After that one, I used the bath towel.

When I returned to the bedroom she was nearly dressed.

I hurriedly got into a fresh shirt.

Doing my necktie, I said, "And how are *your* children, Mrs. Edwards? All's well?"

"You have nothing to say about my children," she said, rumaging through a drawer for gloves. "Jason's gotten himself into Princeton. And Pammy's piano is coming along beautifully. And" —she closed the drawer firmly—"I am bearing the entire cost of their education myself."

I wondered why I had never thought of sending them significant, rotten presents.

I must work that out.

They sure look down their noses at my kids.

While I was putting on my jacket, Pamela looked at me from the bedroom door, hat, veil on head, purse dangling from her forearm, gloves in hand, and she said to me, "Where are you going?"

"Dinner? Aren't we going to dinner?"

"No."

"Oh. Then why did we get dressed?"

"I don't know why 'we' got dressed. I know why I got dressed."

"Why did you get dressed?" I asked, standing there, rather noticeable, I thought, freshly shaven, in a fresh shirt, tie, and jacket.

"I got dressed because we're taping this hour-long panel discussion for national public television at eight o'clock."

"Oh." She hadn't mentioned it before. "Well, then, I'll drive you over, and we'll have dinner after the taping."

"Mark, you know perfectly well that after the taping I will want one drink, a hot tub, and bed."

"Oh." I knew she hadn't mentioned this taping to me before. "Well, I'll drive you over anyway."

"I can take a taxi."

"Why should you? I'm free."

"Mark, there's something you're not understanding."

"I think so."

I waited to be told.

"I'm not Mrs. Mark Edwards."

"You're not?"

"I am Pamela Jensen."

"You're Pamela Jensen."

"There are going to be some other people there—the other panelists. . . ."

"And you don't want to have to say to these other wormy-mouthed creative parasites, 'This is my husband, Mark Edwards . . . '?"

I waited while *other wormy-mouthed creative parasites* disappeared beneath the surface of her skin.

". . . the lovelice columnist?"

"Mark: you're becoming infamous; just slightly infamous."

"Listen, Pamela Jensen, you who write knee-jerk reactions to knee-jerk filums, there's something I haven't told you."

Warily: "Something you haven't told me?"

"Jim Krikorian is actually talking syndication of the DEAR MARK EDWARDS column."

She turned pale.

"Oh, God, no."

"Yes."

The gloves in her hand were shaking.

"You'll ruin me coast to coast."

"Why?" I shouted.

" 'Dear Teensy,' " Pamela quoted, pale and shaking. " 'On your behalf, I have consulted with the leading medical experts on the size of breasts.' " She closed her eyes. " 'Their best advice is that, if there is a body of water near you, such as a river or a lake, you take up rowing a boat as a sport.' " She opened her eyes and stared at me, somberly. " 'They guarantee it will make you row-bust.' "

Pamela always had a most retentive memory.

"What's the matter with that?"

"It's an old joke, Mark. And it's stupid."

"What's so brilliant about what you do? Spending twenty hours a week looking at movies. Is that a normal, grown-up thing to do? You don't write the movies! You don't direct the movies! You don't edit the movies! All you do is write about the movies! All you do is shit all over everybody else's work. Why do you consider yourself such a goddamned intellectual?"

"No one," said Pamela Jensen, "smirks when they hear my name."

"I do!" I said, trying to smirk. *Smirking* is hard to do, on command. "Smirk, smirk," I said, failing. How the hell do you smirk? "Smirk!"

"Good night, Mark."

"How much slapping around do I have to take in one night?" I asked with what I thought was an adequate rhetorical flourish. "First you slap me around because I can't financially support my children and you have to help out. Then you slap me around because there's a chance, just a chance, I might get to earn some real money—"

"Good night, Mark. I'm late. They asked us to be there by seven-fifteen."

I followed her into the living room.

"What do you care? You don't even get paid for appearing on public television. Vanity, vanity!"

The door to the apartment closed, Pamela on the outside, me, all shined up for a night out, on the inside.

"Smirk, smirk," I said to myself. "Slap, slap."

I went into the kitchen and got the ketchup bottle and brought it into the bathroom.

I put *flecks of ketchup* into the bathtub.

Now I have to change my pants before I go out for a hamburger.

I wonder if the cleaner's is open this late at night.

Hope they'll be able to get a little ketchup off the trousers if I bring them right down.

April 17

Dear Mark Edwards:

You've printed alot of letters in your columns from whores charging police harassment.

All they are is poor little unfortunate girls trying to keep body and soul nailed together, right?

Well, that isn't the way to do it.

Listen to me, I've been a downtown dick for twelve years, and let me tell you a few things about these filthy animals you call "ladies."

Mostly, they're filthy, filthy, filthy. Looking at how filthy they are makes you want to throw up.

They're trucking diseases around with them like a sixteen-wheeler carries goods.

Maybe you think spreading syphilis in exchange for a few bucks a trick is a noble thing to do, but I don't.

No sane person comes within ten feet of these "people" if they don't have to.

We instruct the young police officers when they go out to put them in the patrol wagon and bring them in to book them, not even to touch them. Harassment? Anyone who touches those women is a fool.

Next, they seldom give you what you pay for. A sixty-second jerking off, and you've been fucked. If a citizen got so ripped off by a news dealer or a pizza parlor, the cops would be called fast enough.

Most of these street whores don't expect to establish a loyal clientele.

Mostly they're muggers in skirts. They don't consider they've turned a trick until they've stript your wallet, grabbed your watch, and tested to see if the gold fillings in your teeth are loose.

Alot of them never even leave the streets. If they're any good they can separate the usual boozy old boy from his wallet and his watch right there in the doorway with nothing more than a kiss and a hug.

If they're not that deft of finger yet, then they just back their "client" into whatever pickpocket they're working with.

Let's have a little truth here.

I know it's news to you newspaper liberals, but such things as prostitution and pickpocketing are against the law.

You want to change the law, go ahead and change it.

Until you do, don't print any more crap about us cops harassing people when we're only doing our duty.

Captain Midnight
(Lt. Steve Kroyak)

April 20

Dear Lieutenant Kroyak:

Hogwash.

If you've spent twelve years on the police force and can write a letter like yours of the seventeenth to me then you're either terribly naïve or terribly dishonest.

I don't think anyone can spend twelve years on the force and be that naïve.

You cops could rid this country of prostitution, pickpocketing, and mugging within a week, if you wanted to, just by enforcing the laws that are already available to you.

And don't give me any hogwash about our crappy court system.

Such crimes as prostitution, pickpocketing, and mugging are committed over and over again by known perpetrators in a predictable place at a predictable time.

Yeah, Captain Midnight, "Let's have a little truth here."

It's not the court system that's preventing our streets from being cleaned up—it's the payoff system.

These crimes wouldn't exist in our city streets if the cops weren't getting a healthy slice of the action.

The arrests you make are meaningless, and only made to convince the public you're doing something to earn your pay.

And those arrests are highly selective.

You only pick up the girls with the weakest pimps.

You have evidence of procuring, assault, battery, bribery (and tax evasion) against every pimp in your district.

How many pimps have you picked up in the last year?

Go grease your Cadillac, Captain Midnight.

Love Never Faileth,
Mark Edwards

April 18

Dear Mark Edwards:

It took a lot of effort on my part to get into this Correctional Institution (see above Correctional Institution), which effort I expended willingly as I had heard this particular Correctional Institution has the best library in the state Correctional Institutional system.

Alas, after the past several weeks of studious investigation, I must report that the library in this particular Correctional Institution is far from adequate.

To cite an example you will appreciate, not only does this library not have Edward Gibbon's *The Decline and Fall of the Roman Empire,* it doesn't even have C. S. Forester's Horatio Hornblower series.

This is an enormous disappointment to me, as I like reading more than I like anything else.

And I fear, having gone to all this effort to matriculate at this particular Correctional Institution, that I may be here for a good long time.

Voracious
(Ella Gray)

April 20

Dear Ms. Gray:

What are you in for, counterfeit library cards?

Come off it, babe, you're not in a "Correctional Institution"— you're in the can.

And to get there you committed an offense against some person, persons, or Society in general—which includes me.

Frankly, I don't feel like working my head off at honest labor to support you, while you sit back on your bunk reading books I haven't time to read.

I agree with you: something's wrong here.

There are too many of us who would like to take a few years off while Society keeps us warm and fed, with access to a good library.

My heart doesn't bleed for you.

Love Never Faileth,
Mark Edwards

(April 21)

Dear Mark Edwards:

Although this correctional institution has the reputation of having the best library in the state, for a correctional institution, it simply isn't true.

The library is far from adequate.

As an example, it not only doesn't have Gibbon's *Decline and Fall of the Roman Empire,* it doesn't even have C. S. Forester's Horatio Hornblower series.

Voracious

Dear Voracious:

I'm glad to be able to ask the readers of this column to send any extra books they have to Fort Langdon Correctional Institution, Fort Langdon, c/o Librarian.

Thanks for letting us know about this problem.

Dear Mark Edwards:

I've been a city police officer for 12 years and I have something to say in response to the letters written by prostitutes which have appeared in your column charging the police with "harassment."

Most of the prostitutes I've had to deal with have been filthy, diseased rip-off artists and pickpockets.

No sane person would come within 20 feet of these people if they didn't have to. Harassment? Anyone who touches those women is a fool.

By no stretch of the imagination are they "ladies."

Prostitution is against the law. We police officers are only doing our duty.

If Society wants to change the law, and make prostitution a legitimate business, then we will be relieved of our duty to arrest prostitutes.

Captain Midnight

Dear Captain Midnight:

Glad to see you agree with us.

Prostitution, it is said, is the world's oldest profession (frankly, I always thought apple-picking is the world's oldest profession, as that is the first Old Testament report of work being done) and it has almost always been against the law, and yet here it is, flourishing better than ever, complete with terrible criminal violence and a vast array of horrible social diseases.

Decriminalize prostitution and Society will be able to stamp out the diseases, in time, and rid the world of much violence.

Is that what you're saying, Captain Midnight?

Dear Mark Edwards:

I wrote you before—signing myself as "Suffering Lady"—asking how I could get it across to my husband that I like a little rough-and-tumble in our sex play.

Well, last night I did exactly as you said and took him aside and showed him some of the things I had purchased for us, boots and the whip and all, and did he get excited! It was marvelous!

I want to thank you for your good advice, and let other people know that You, Too, Can Have a Bigger, More Fulfilling Sex Life if you're just patient, kind, and considerate.

(No Longer) Suffering Lady

Dear (No Longer) Suffering Lady:

It's always amazing what can be accomplished when one person really tries to communicate with another.

Dear Mark Edwards:

I'm really worried about my wife.

She spends her whole life—as many as 20 hours a week—watching movies.

Is this a normal, grown-up thing to do?

What's worse is that she seems to feel that watching so many movies makes her some kind of an intellectual. She comments on the movies, and criticizes them—as if anybody cares what she thinks.

Now I have a real opportunity for a big promotion in my work situation, and it's pretty obvious to me she couldn't care less.

Whatever I do, either it's not "intellectual" enough—or, more likely, it doesn't come up to the fantasies she gets off the silver screen.

Any ideas?

L.N.F.

Dear L.N.F.:

Get rich and get rid of her.

6.

April 22

TO: Mark Edwards

FROM: James Krikorian, Managing Editor

Mark, you're wonderful!

How the hell can you make an *issue*, for Chrissake, out of whether prostitutes are ladies? And keep the "issue" going so long?

Keep it up!

Put the twenty-eighth down for lunch with me and Owen Hatch, of the News/Features Syndicate.

They're interested in taking on the DEAR MARK EDWARDS column.

And screw the front office. What do they know?

April 22

Dear ME:

It felt like Pamela was already staring at me (very sourly, I must say) before I even came through the front door.

She was sitting in a living-room chair in her housecoat, her feet curled up under her, yesterday's newspaper crumpled on the floor.

It took me a moment to remember what I had done—this time.

"Good evening, sunshine," I said, brightly. "Beautiful spring night. How's tricks?"

Horseradish, mixed with lemon juice and Worcestershire sauce —that was the quality of scowl I was getting.

She said: " 'Get rich and get rid of her,' uh?"

"Oh. That."

"That. So one of your readers' wives spends twenty hours a week looking at movies and her husband writes in to ask if that is a normal, grown-up thing to do?"

"Funny, some of the letters I get."

"Funny, some of the letters you write."

"Write?"

"Right."

"Gee. You caught me."

"Is sitting in a room alone, writing letters to yourself, a 'normal, grown-up thing to do'?"

"What are we going to do about dinner?"

"Ketchup in the bathtub isn't bad enough," she said.

"*Flecks of ketchup*," I amended. "I think it's funny."

"I think it's sick."

" 'Anyone who thinks he isn't mad in a mad world is suffering a madness.' "

"Who said that?"

"Saul Bellow. *Henderson the Rain King*."

"Is that exactly what he said?"

"More or less. My memory isn't as retentive as yours."

"Someone must care about my film criticism," she said. "*Hawthorne's* pays me quite a lot for it."

"A mere pittance. A trifle."

Her eyes widened. "You mean 'a mere pittance' compared to

what you think you can earn running that smut column coast to coast?"

"And around the world."

She stood up and approached me, slowly.

I have no idea why I was half expecting a moment of tenderness.

I guess I've been reading too many kooky letters.

"The letter in your column says I couldn't care less whether you get a big promotion in your work situation."

I put my arms (well, my hands, my forearms) out to her.

"You mean you do care?"

"I care a great deal," she said, softly. Sweetly, still a few feet away from me, her face turned up to me, she said: "I—despise—the—whole—thought—of—it."

Not even an exclamation.

Simple declarative.

She turned toward the bedroom door.

"The Chalmers' have invited us to dinner," she said.

"I didn't know that."

"I'll make your excuses."

"I'm not going?"

"And, please," Pamela said. "No ketchup in the bathtub tonight, okay? The man in the cleaner's shop told me you had ketchup all over your pants."

"Jeez," I said. "No confidentiality anywhere anymore."

"Oh yes there is," Pamela said. "I didn't tell him you got ketchup all over your pants while pouring it into the bathtub."

"Flecking it."

"I'm a very loyal wife."

"I'll say."

From the bedroom she said, "What does 'L.N.F.' mean?"

"What?"

"The letter from yourself was signed 'L.N.F.' What do the initials mean?"

Standing in the living-room alone, I shrugged. "Love Never Faileth."

"What?"

"Love Never Faileth," I said.

"Who made that up?"

"I did," I said. "I think."

"Catchy," she said. "Catchy."

So again I write my journal in a silent apartment before going out for another hamburger.

Another letter to myself.

April 21

Dear Mark:

Over the years I've wondered about you so often, and so fondly. It never entered my head you would still be here, in the same city, working for the same newspaper—although I will admit that when I came back to the city late last year I looked through your newspaper several days, to spot your by-line, if it were there. In my heart, I've felt sure you'd be riding a horse in Montana, or, at the very least, running a motel or an orange juice stand or something near the baseball Spring Training Camps in Florida. Anyhow, that's how I've thought of you, wishing you well, thinking of you doing something you really wanted to do.

I like your column, dear Mark Edwards. It seems you've turned into a wise, warm, and witty man—a good deal less uptight than you were during those few days we were married.

I never have been able to understand what there was about me that always made you so nervous. I think of our little marriage with guilt. I have the impression I sort of took you over for my own purposes—whatever they were—when you needed time to swim a river, ride a horse, climb a mountain. I can't forgive myself for the restlessness I always remember from your big, neat body —even after our making love, time and again. We were so young, Mark, and each of us beautiful.

Of course, I've thought of calling you since I first noticed your column, but I figured that would be too much of a shock, for both of us.

Everyone else in the world seems to be writing you, so I thought I would, too.

Will my letter be lost in traffic, or answered by an assistant? or not answered at all?

With the warmest, friendliest feelings in the world for you,
I remain,

Mari

April 23

Dear Mari:

In joy from hearing from you (and in complete confusion—why
aren't I rushing over to you, instead of sitting here at a type-
writer?—the whole thing is a shock) I am answering you too
quickly, too automatically, as if yours were any other letter.

It's just that these days all I'm doing is writing letters. No social life, no romantic life, not even a fantasy life (except vicari-
ously through my correspondents!).

Forgive me for answering you with a letter, but that's what
I'm down to—that's how I relate to people now.

I even write letters to myself!

It doesn't seem a very grown-up way to live, does it?

I did go "ride a horse" after you left me. (Actually, I worked
as a box boy in a department store in Dayton, Ohio, pumped gas
in Georgia, and was a bank teller in Eugene, Oregon—so much
for historic, romantic American images.) Frankly, it took me
much more time to accept your having left me than all the time
we spent together.

You did it so softly, so sweetly. Without complaint, criticism,
a harsh word, suddenly you weren't there—when somehow I
knew you wouldn't be.

By the way, if memory serves, I still owe you twenty-five
dollars and thirteen cents—your share of what I got selling our
furniture. I broke up our little apartment about three weeks
later.

You referred to our "little marriage."

I refer to our "little apartment."

The French probably have a proper phrase for what happened
to us.

I don't.

Are you still beautiful?

Of course.

I must come look.

Just give me a few minutes, or days, or whatever it takes.
I have letters to write.

Love Never Faileth,
Mark

April 20

Mark Edwards:
Just wait until I get out. Just you wait.

The Fried-Ass Face-Slasher
(Jumbo Dondershine)

P.S. I peed on this letter.

April 23

Dear Mr. Dondershine:
So did I.

Love Never Faileth,
Mark Edwards

April 21

Dear Mark Edwards:
A month ago, Silva (you know, Silva Mellon? She signed her
letter to you as "The Ladies") wrote you a letter I guess about
how the cops are always hassling us?

We found your letter to her and your column torn out of the
paper among her stuff.

She went around talking about let's unionize and even hire
a public relations guy for all of us and all this crazy talk.

Anyway, I want you to know that three nights ago Silva was
found under a parked car with a knife through her lung.

So that's enough of that shit.

The Ladies
(Frankie Gordon)

April 23

Dear Ms. Gordon:
I'm sorry.
What can I say?
You're in a rough business.
Why don't you and some of the other ladies take this as a clue

as to what might happen to you as long as you stay in that business, and get the hell out of it?

Love Never Faileth,
Mark Edwards

April 19

Dear Mark Edwards:

Our Committee would appreciate your expressing your views in your column concerning violence on television.

Our view is that constant violence on television encourages increasing violence in our lives and is largely responsible for the worldwide annual increase in crime rates.

Lillian Odell, Pres.
Television-Terrible
Committee

April 23

Dear Ms. Odell:

I think anyone responsible for depicting violence on television should be kicked in the head, have his eyes gouged, his nose chopped off, be run through with a sword, and shot in the left hip.

Love Never Faileth,
Mark Edwards

April 25

TO: Mark Edwards

FROM: James Krikorian, Managing Editor

Owen Hatch, of News/Features Syndicate, has switched to a later plane from Chicago, so change that lunch date the twenty-eighth to dinner, same day. Seven-thirty all right? We'll meet in the bar at Saunders'.

April 24

Dear Mark Edwards:

Growing up, I was always told that a man's sexual ability disappears after thirty, or fifty, or seventy, or something.

Well, mine hasn't, and I'm seventy-eight!

I think you should print this testimonial to the testes, for the sake of younger people.

It might take some of the urgency out of their sexual demands, if you know what I mean.

There's plenty of time, son. Plenty of time.

> The Hotcha Grandpo
> (Oliver Brackbill)

April 26

Dear Mr. Brackbill:

Coming to you under separate cover is our Golden Prophylactic Award.

Don't get into trouble.

> Love Never Faileth,
> Mark Edwards

(April 27)

Dear Mark Edwards:

Our Committee would appreciate your expressing your views in your column concerning violence on television.

Our view is that constant violence on television encourages increasing violence in our lives and is largely responsible for the worldwide annual increase in crime rates.

> Television-Terrible
> Committee

Dear Television-Terrible Committee:

Your idea that violence on television causes us to be more and more violence-prone must be correct, because before television all we had as literary influences was the Bible, fairy tales, and the works of Shakespeare, and we sure were gory then.

Dear Mark Edwards:

A while ago one of the girls here on the street wrote you a letter signing herself "The Ladies" saying as how the cops are always hassling us and running us down to the station and you wrote back suggesting we business girls try to unionize.

Well, she went around talking about us unionizing and even hiring a public relations person for all of us, and a few nights ago she was found under a parked car with a knife through her lung.

I thought you should know.

> The B-Girls

Dear B-Girls:

Why don't you go on strike?

Incidentally, I have asked the Commissioner of Police for your area if this murder is being thoroughly investigated, and he has assured me it is. I expect this newspaper will carry daily reports on the progress of the investigation.

Dear Mark Edwards:

At 78, I can tell you a man's sexual ability does not leave him—as I'd always been told.

The young should know this, so they won't always be in such a damned fool hurry.

The Hotcha Grandpo

Dear Hotcha Grandpo:

I've always heard it's like any other muscle—stop using it, and it stops working.

Dear Mark Edwards:

I have a son in military school, and we're simply not hearing from him.

Of course, I suppose he's still upset about his mother and me being divorced, but that happened four or five years ago.

Recently I have sent him a little extra cash, thinking the response would be instantaneous, but so far, no word from him.

Loving Dad

Dear Loving Dad:

These situations are always difficult.

I suspect if you had the support of your ex-wife—the boy's mother— in urging him toward you emotionally, things would be easier all around.

Don't give up on him.

Dear Mark Edwards:

A long time ago, a boy and I were very much in love with each other. In fact, we were married for a short while.

Recently, I have discovered we are living in the same city. He's fairly well known.

After hesitating a long time, I wrote him a little note, and he answered happily enough (my return address was on the letter).

We don't seem to be rushing to see each other, as two old friends normally would.

It's hard to know what to think about this situation.

Old Friend

Dear Old Friend:

Of course it's hard to know what to think of this situation.

A lot of water must have gone under that bridge.

Doubtless he is deeply involved in a completely different life now—as probably you are yourself.

You mention, almost casually, you had been married to each other "a short while."

Is it possible he has never told anyone he was married to you?

And, of course, there must have been some reason why you separated in the first place.

Is it ever wise to try to go back?

Sometimes it is best to leave memories alone—as memories.

April 29

Dear ME:

Jim Krikorian and Owen Hatch of the News/Features Syndicate were already belly-up to the bar at Saunders' by the time I got there, a little after seven-thirty.

My guess was they had been there awhile.

Jim introduced us, referring to me as "Our Fuckin' Correspondent, Dear Mark Edwards—the Guru of Gonorrhea."

"Very funny, Jim."

It was conceivable I could have been a Foreign Correspondent: if it hadn't been for that damned airport fire; if UPI hadn't thought I did such a splendid job writing about it; if book publishers hadn't been so stupid in thinking books about airport fires wouldn't sell in airports!

People love to believe they have something to be scared about at airports.

Else why are airport bars always so full?

"The lovelice columnist," I said.

Owen Hatch was just as I expected, only a bit more so: the best of the American salesman class, hale and hearty, florid in face, chummy, wet-eyed, a well-dressed, prosperous fat body which laughed easily, each laugh invariably ending in a strangling smoker's cough.

"May I call you *dear* for short?" he asked.

Jim thought that very funny.

I guessed they had been drinking together since about six.

"Our table's not ready yet, Mark," Jim said. "You have time for a drink or three. What'll you have?"

"Gin and Alka-Seltzer," I said, trying to add to their hilarity.

"Gin and tonic," Jim said to the barman.

"Funny man," Owen Hatch said, choking. "Funny, funny."

"Bitter lemon," I amended, to the barman.

"Mark, you know, is married to Pamela Jensen," Jim told Owen. "The film critic."

"Oh?"

Owen's eyes were as transparent as a cash register's window. Up popped several tentative figures before the final sum total. A quick calculation of whether and how he could use the fact that I am Pamela Jensen's husband to sell the DEAR MARK EDWARDS column around the country, and a final rejection of the idea. I could see it all. No. The name Pamela Jensen is too associated with intellectualism to be useful in selling the kind of shit I'm doing. Might even be harmful.

"Of *Hawthorne's* magazine," Jim added, unnecessarily. "By the way, Mark, I saw Pamela today."

"You did?"

Jim's eyes swallowed something. (It's always weird being an hour and a half behind other people's heavy drinking: one's perceptions are still working acutely, while their defenses are a little gone.) There was something he wasn't telling me, and wasn't going to tell me.

"Just to say hello," he said.

"Here, barman!" Owen put his empty glass on the bar. "Where's Mr. Edwards' drink? This is Mark Edwards, the syndicated columnist."

The barman looked at me as he would at an object.

To my surprise he did know who I was. I mean, am.

"We're in the same business," I said to him. "Advice to the depressive."

Jesus. What I said is true, I'm becoming barman to the world! Owen's glance at me was quick, and worried.

"Mark's getting so much mail now," Jim told Owen, "he says the Post Office is thinking of giving him his own zip code!"

Owen was still thinking. He had heard something he hadn't liked.

"What percentage of the letters you get do you use in your column?" Jim asked.

"A very small percentage."

"What are most of them like?"

"Many of them are unreadable. I can't read the handwriting, or they're totally incoherent, written by real sickies, or drunks, or people on one drug or other. You know, people thinking they have something to say, crying out for human contact, help, attention. I get a lot of mail from people in institutions, you know, prisons, hospitals, mental hospitals."

I tried my drink.

"A terrific percentage of the letters are from people who want me to publicize something—anything from their group's bingo party to a major recording company hoping I'll work in a reference to their latest LP. I never mention anything of the sort, but they never give up."

Owen Hatch was still listening very carefully.

"There are letters from people who want to, need to, have to share their problems with someone, anyone, in their scatter-brained, or, I should say, scatter-shot attempt to find a solution. And there are those who make up problems, just to have something to write, just to see if you'll print their letter, for the thrill of seeing whatever name they sign in print."

Owen was half looking away, listening, drinking.

"And," I continued, "there are letters from people who have found solutions, nice letters, happy letters. People who want to share good news, good experiences, their opinions with other people."

Owen Hatch said, "It doesn't sound like a very happy job, to me."

"Sure it is," I answered. "Just like almost everyone else in the world right now, I'm dealing with human beings on little slips of paper." I let that sink in a moment. "It's perpetually amazing to me," I said, "how well so many people write when they're writing about something they care about—when they really have something to say."

"Is that so?" said Jim. "Have you ever written a letter to a column like DEAR MARK EDWARDS, Owen? I mean, when you were a kid, or something? Did you, Mark?"

We each testified we had never written in to anything like the DEAR MARK EDWARDS column.

That buoyed everybody up.

"The readers love a column like this," Jim said. "Even the ones who'd never think of writing a letter. They love to look into other people's lives, get the dirt about real people, see that other people have problems, too."

Owen Hatch said, "I know."

"And the great thing about Mark," Jim continued, selling the salesman, "is that he raises these stupid questions to the level of *issues*." He laughed. "Like all the prostitutes today announcing they're on strike."

"They did?" I asked. "They are?"

"Didn't you know?" Jim said. "Didn't you read the P.M.?"

"I was too busy," I said.

"All the prostitutes in town. They're on strike. From your column, yesterday. That broad—what's her name?"

"Silva Mellon," I said.

"Yeah. Silva Mellon. She wrote you a letter and somebody murdered her and yesterday in your column you suggested they all go on strike. And they did." Jim put his hand on Owen's shoulder, laughing. "On the very day old Owen here comes to town! Poor old Owen!"

Poor old Owen grinned ruefully.

"At least Mari's is open," he muttered.

"Yeah," Jim said. "We'll go there after dinner."

"Marie's?" I said.

"Where the hell's our table?"

Jim caught the eye of the headwaiter at the door.

"Marie's?" I said.

"Mari's," answered Owen. "M-a-r-i-apostrophe-s. There's one in London and one in Los Angeles and one here. We don't have one in Chicago, yet."

M-a-r-i-apostrophe-s?

"You don't know about Mari's?" Jim said. "Some swinging journalist you are. Really *au courant*, right, Mark? There's nothing you don't know! I'm proud of ya!"

I was embarrassing my managing editor. To hell with it.

"What's Mari's?" I asked.

"A nightclub!" Jim expressed some exasperation with his Fuckin' Correspondent. "Opened about the first of the year. There's nothin' like it in the whole world! Let's eat."

"Except in London and Los Angeles," Owen muttered. "Not in Chicago."

Is it conceivable Mari is in the nightclub business? Possible? Probable?

There was enough of a chance of it that I sat at the table, staring at the menu, feeling slightly sick and shaky.

I did not want to see Mari, *my Mari*, after dinner. I didn't even want there to be a chance of it. The slightest chance. Not after all these years. Not just like that: after dinner. Not in the presence of Jim Krikorian and Owen Hatch.

Around my ears swirled their boyish, drunken tales of Mari and Mari's nightclubs.

"Excuse me," I said. "I promised to make a phone call."

They looked at me in surprise and dismay.

I wasn't doing very much to help Jim sell my column to the syndicate.

In the phone booth I scanned the Yellow Pages for a nightclub with a half-decent address. I hadn't been in one in years. I had a poor impression of all of them.

"Good evening. This is Judson speaking."

"Oh. Judson?"

"May I help you?"

"Yes." I hesitated. "This is Mark Edwards."

"Yes, sir?"

"You know, Mark Edwards? The syndicated columnist? News/ Features Syndicate?"

There was a pause.

I could hear the prick smiling.

"Yes, Mr. Edwards."

Never again would I say this-is-Mark-Edwards-you-know-the-syndicated-columnist.

Except in an emergency.

(And I wasn't even syndicated yet!)

"If you have a good table, three of us will be by in an hour or two."

"Yes, Mr. Edwards."

"Will you have a good table?"

"We will, sir. For you."

"Thank you."

I hung up.

Then picked up the receiver and slammed it down.

Damned fool!

Back in the dining room I discovered they had ordered me a martini.

I cleared my throat.

Jim and Owen looked at me.

"You'll love Judson's," I said.

They said nothing.

I said, more softly, "I'm really looking forward to taking you both to Judson's."

"What's Judson's?" Owen asked.

"A nightclub," said Jim.

"Great little place," I said.

Owen looked at Jim.

"I thought we were going to Mari's."

"Oh, hell," I said. "You'd never get in that place. Too popular. Jam-packed. Hot."

Jim was looking at me through squinted eyes.

"Oh, I'm sorry, Jim," I said. "Do you have reservations at Mari's?"

He said, "I thought the three of us—the managing editor of the local newspaper, the managing editor of News/Features Syndicate, and *Dear* Mark Edwards—would be impressive enough at the door—"

"I have reservations at Judson's," I said.

Over dinner, conversation was more serious, and somewhat subdued.

"Mark, Owen says he has sixty papers already interested in taking on the DEAR MARK EDWARDS column."

Sixty newspapers!

"A hundred." Owen was disdainful of his roast beef, which wasn't up to what he was used to in Chicago. "I think we'll be beginning with a hundred."

A hundred newspapers!

I said, "That's nice."

I discovered that 50 percent of what the syndicate paid for the DEAR MARK EDWARDS column would be going to my newspaper. To Monroe Lipton, Publisher. The Board of Directors, stockholders all. Other stockholders from Saskatchewan to

New South Wales, who hadn't seen an edition of the newspaper in years, probably would be surprised to know they owned a slice of the column and had never heard of *Dear* Mark Edwards. And into the pay packet of the newspaper's chief telephone operator, who snapped her gum when answering the phone . . .

"Great," I said.

(The roast beef was better than the hamburger I had been getting used to.)

. . . for which the newspaper would supply me with an assistant.

The singularity of this was so pronounced, one might even refer to it as *a* assistant.

"Terrific," I said.

We went on to Judson's, where the table was small and sticky, right in front of a band that blared, and where the drinks came fast and watery.

We dropped Owen off in a taxi at his hotel.

"This is terrific," I said to Jim Krikorian. "Syndication! Wow! Thanks very much, Jim."

"Prick," he said. "Shithead. Bastard. You codicil to an obscenity!"

I thought answering such definite statements futile.

He rolled out of the cab at his town house saying, "Now I have to take that bastard to Mari's tomorrow night!" He slammed the door and stood on the sidewalk, shouting (sobbing, one might say): "And you're not invited!"

A very expensive evening.

Hell, I can afford it! ME! Mark Edwards!

7.

May 1

TO: Mark Edwards

FROM: Monroe Lipton, Publisher

Jim Krikorian tells us that News/Features Syndicate has taken on your marvelous, lively column, DEAR MARK EDWARDS, and I want to express to you the congratulations and best wishes from myself, Mrs. Lipton, and the Board of Directors of this newspaper.

You have always been one of our favorite people, Mark. Nothing is more pleasing than to see one of our own succeed, as we always knew you would—especially after you won that UPI Award a few years back for your excellent coverage of that fire at the airport.

Just last night, Mrs. Lipton suggested calling your wife, to invite you both over to the house for dinner, sometime soon.

April 30

Dear Dad:

Thanks for sending me the $5 bill.

With it I bought a box of crackers and a Dick Tracy Decoder Ring.

Mark II

May 2

Dear Mark:

Nice to hear from you.

Do you know that your sister refers to you as "Military Markey, the Curious Cadet"? She also refers to your stepmother as *that woman you're living with,* and me, of course, as Dear Daddy Dodderer.

I guess you're trying to tell me that, as far as largesse goes, five bucks isn't very much.

When I was a kid, if anybody gave me five bucks, I would have set up an apartment and taken out a marriage license.

As a matter of fact, I think that's just about what I did do.

Never fear. Things are looking up.

News/Features has just picked up the column I'm doing, DEAR MARK EDWARDS, for syndication. Your dear, doddering Daddy is now to appear in one hundred newspapers, coast to coast.

Check your local scandal sheet for that glittering by-line which is your very own name!

If this keeps up, next year maybe I'll be able to send you seven dollars and fifty cents!

And if you think this isn't important, let me tell you—after a lifetime of working for this newspaper, never having had anything more warming from the publisher than a zero-Celsius who-are-you "Good morning"—I'm now told I'm one of his favorite people, and his wife is *thinking* of inviting us to dinner!

Of course they're getting 50 percent of my income from the column, and that ought to be worth a plate of chicken-and-peas any day, right?

My new prosperity is causing me to think a happy thought about this summer, but I'm not ready to report what it is, yet.

I find it's rather late to start making a plan, and I don't know if what I want to do is possible, at this late date.

But I'll give you a hint.

Your Dad turns forty in July.

Don't let such a long time go by without our hearing from you again.

> Love Never Faileth,
> Dad

May 2

Dear ME:

There was something new in Pamela's eyes tonight, when I came in. Defeat? I wouldn't like to think so. Curiosity? I had told her nothing about my meeting with Jim Krikorian and Owen Hatch. But today was the first day the DEAR MARK EDWARDS column appeared with the "Syndicated by News/Features" slug on it. More of an openness? willingness? acceptance?

I hope so.

I said nothing.

I turned on the record player. A Liza Minnelli LP.

Pamela said, "I have to do another public television panel show tonight. I was hoping you'd drive me over, and we can have supper later."

"I don't want to stand around a drafty television studio." I shrugged. "I find it embarrassing."

She sighed. I knew what was in her mind. *You're now Mark Edwards—syndicated columnist. You don't have to stand around anywhere.*

"Merriam called," she said.

"Merriam called you?"

"She was calling you. I just got the brunt of her fury."

"Hardly fair for an ex-wife to yell at a current wife. There are rules about such things. Remind me to send her a copy of *Manners Among Wives, Past and Present.*"

"Merriam doesn't yell. Neither do I."

"I know."

"She expresses concern. She expresses distress."

"What did she express this time?"

"Anger."

"Oh, joy."

"Quiet anger."

"Not quiet enough." Liza Minnelli was beginning "Raggedy Ann and Raggedy Andy." *Marvelous Mari and Merry Mark.* And fifty dollars and twenty-six cents' worth of furniture. "I'm supposed to ask why Merriam is quietly angry at me, right?"

"Your advice, in your column the other day, to 'Loving Dad,' who hasn't heard from his son in military school."

"Oh. That one."

"You wrote something like, 'If you had the support of your ex-wife in urging him toward you emotionally, things would be easier all around, but don't give up on the boy.'" Pamela had used an "old boy's tone" in quoting me. "Really, Mark, even I knew that was a phony letter."

I thought how concerned . . . distressed . . . angry both Merriam and Pamela would be if they knew the next letter in the column, *Dear Old Friend, Sometimes it is best to leave memories alone—as memories* was also phony. Marvelous Mari and Merry Mark.

They might even yell.

That would be refreshing.

Pamela said, "I'm delighted for your new success, Mark. Really I am."

"All of a sudden you like smut?"

"I think you could accomplish a lot of good through that column."

"Thank you."

"Not, however, if, in your attempt to be funny, you answer questions as stupidly as you did the letter from the Television-Terrible Committee. 'Before television all we had as literary influences was the Bible, fairy tales, and the works of Shakespeare'"—And Pamela put on a yuck-bumpkin accent—"'and we sure were gory then.'"

"Ow," I said. "Is there anything worse than being married to a professional critic with a retentive memory?"

"'Ow' is what I said when I read it."

"It happens to be true, and it happens to be funny."

"But it's not what you really think."

"Violence is in the People, Pamela." (Here I was talking about the People, and I hadn't had a drink all day.) "Not in their implements of communication."

"It's not right to use the column to swing out at people, like Merriam and me, who can't swing back at you in the same forum."

"Sure you can. Anyone can write me a letter." Mari wrote me a letter. "Almost everyone does."

"Are you coming to the television studio with me?"

"No. There's some work I want to do."

The work I want to do is to write ME.

Not only am I writing letters to myself, nowadays, I'm beginning to have fantasies, too, just like my readers. The occupational hazards of a lovelice columnist.

The fantasy attacking me—the wildest of all wild sexual fantasies—is that I can return to my youthful moments, youthful feelings, with Mari—*each of us beautiful,* as she wrote.

Why can't I take my own advice? It is best to leave *memories alone—as memories.*

You cannot twice have first love—even, especially, with the same person.

Reading the above platitudes makes me realize I am well suited to my lovelice job. I am not superior to it at all.

I, too, am loveshorn.

I had gone into a stationery store to buy a pencil to write a poem. (In those days, each poem I wrote had to be written with a new pencil. One pencil a poem. The pencil had to be fresh, virginal. No previous thought ever could have flowed down its length to the reality of the word on paper, to sully or even influence the present thought of that particular poem. My poems were pure.) (It's still true. These days my columns are written on an electric typewriter, and there is no question that what I write is heavily influenced by the Edison Electric Company. My current muse is Reddy Kilowatt.)

Mari was at the counter, in a worn duffel coat and old, scuffed shoes, ordering engraved stationery for herself. Her skin was a color and texture I had never seen before. It belonged on an angel, or some other, even more exalted heavenly creature, and even looking at it was breaking through the walls of existence, transcending life as it is, reality, an essentential experience, a clear view of forever. Her hair was honey. The salesgirl was stooped over the counter, writing out the order, and Mari looked along the counter at me. Her weird, violet eyes focused on me in three beats: first, they looked; instantly they grew wider; they narrowed.

I took the few steps to her and put my hand on hers, on the glass counter. A sample of the stationery she was ordering was also on the counter. It was feminine and expensive—for someone dressed as scruffily as she was.

I read the order upside down as the salesgirl made it out.

"No," I said. "The stationery should say Mari Edwards."

The salesgirl looked up. "I thought you said you wanted the stationery engraved in the name Mari Ostroy."

"Edwards is her married name," I said of the girl I had never seen before in my life. "She forgot."

"I take it you two haven't been married long?"

"We've been married forever," I said. "Sometimes it's just hard to remember—we've been married that long. What address did you give, Mari?"

Eyebrows had risen over violet eyes.

The salesgirl read off an address.

"No, that's wrong," I said. "We're moving soon. Don't bother with that address. In fact, don't bother with the order at all. We'll come back to you after we get a new address."

Hand in hand we walked out of the store.

On the sidewalk, hands in the pockets of her coat, Mari said, "I hope you know that salesgirl in there thinks you just recaptured an escapee from an institution."

"What that salesgirl in there actually saw," I said, "was the beginning of one of history's great love stories."

I kissed her. I kissed Mari.

"Don't you like being Mari Edwards?" I asked.

"Of course I do, John."

"My name's not John."

"Joe. Tom. Charlie."

"My name's not Joe, Tom, or Charlie."

"Tell me the truth. Did I just escape from an institution?"

"I don't know. Maybe. How would I know? I never saw you before."

I went into her pocket and dug out her hand and began to walk with her through the black and white March.

"You can read it off the marriage license," I said. "My name."

For a marriage that would last three months, the rest of March, through April, May, and into June, we had no doubt about what we were doing in getting married. No doubt, no question, no hesitation. Neither of us had had a life before (has either of us had a life since?). Our "little marriage" exists as a little island, a slice of hard-boiled egg in a vast sea of mock turtle soup.

"Mark." She read it off the application for the marriage license. "Mark, Mark, Mark."

We rented a loft that afternoon, bought a secondhand mattress, dragged it up four flights of stairs to the loft, and put it on the floor near the radiators.

Then I took off my jacket and sweater and shirt and T-shirt.

"What are you doing?" she asked.

I was sitting on the floor, taking off my sneakers.

"We're going to make love," I said.

"Now?"

"Rightio."

"We just went through a lot of crap to get signed up for marriage."

I looked up at her, still in her duffel coat.

"I'm not marrying you just to make love," I said. "And I'm not making love with you just to get married. They're two separable instincts."

Violet eyes glopped me again.

"Get the idea?"

She jumped. "Yeah!" She grabbed off her coat and tossed it toward the door.

When she had her shirt and bra off, I stared her straight in the nipples and said, "Have you ever fucked before?"

"Not really."

"Not really?"

"No. Not really."

I considered where all the various lines of sexual relativity were, or, outreaching, might be.

"I guess I haven't either," I said. "Really."

Each of us beautiful, she wrote.

I never told her I was going to be a great journalist and she never told me she was going to be a great schoolteacher. I guess we were both right not to make promises.

Sweet hours of lovemaking.

I was a copy boy at the newspaper.

"Money is freedom," she shortly said. "There are things we want to do."

She never said what we wanted to do. I would lie awake nights on our mattress trying to think what we wanted to do.

Apparently she thought I wanted to, needed to, ride a horse and swim in rivers. I was nineteen. (At nearly forty, I can tell you no one needs to be a box boy in a department store in Dayton, Ohio, pump gas in Georgia, or be a bank teller in Eugene, Oregon.) What made me nervous? She had this idea of *forward motion,* that we were going somewhere, or should be going somewhere, had a goal or ought to have a goal. (She was ambitious? She should have known, regarding me, that writing poetry and being ambitious are usually mutually exclusive. To be a great writer-of-headlines [which craft exercises the skill of poetry to its highest degree]. Maybe a baseball writer. [Goddamn that airport fire and UPI!]) I loved looking at her and touching her and playing with her. With all this, what else was I supposed to plan, do, think, be? *Tomorrow* was in her silences, and came to be in my silences, too. What in hell was *tomorrow?* However hard I tried, I could achieve no vision of it. I could not pretend to know about *tomorrow.* (The only times I had ever thought of *tomorrow* as a specific thing was once a year—the day before baseball season opened!)

Dimly, softly, sweetly, without a word from her, I came to understand that without *tomorrow,* tomorrow would be without Mari.

"Money is freedom," she said.

She left her teachers' training courses, lied about her age (not very convincingly, I suspect, but who cared, under the circumstances?) and got a job as a cocktail waitress. Her work uniform was a pair of shiny green panties and a lace bra with tassels dangling from her tits. (Odd—the only thing I thought excessive about that costume, disturbing, was her ridiculous high-heeled shoes!)

Some nights I would go to the lounge early (every night I would be there to walk her home) and have a beer and watch her. Even in that wretched, dark, dirty, smelly place she appeared as a sunbeam, so prideful, healthful, unselfconscious she was, in moving her bod in those stupid shoes, doing her putrid duties, serving more and more poison to the dying and already dead.

But what were we making money for? What were we saving money for? We had our mattress, a rickety table, two old chairs, a few pans—fifty dollars and twenty-six cents' worth of furniture. What was I supposed to do?

Have a great, lifelong plan.

An ambition.

My ambition was to love Mari.

Maybe it still is.

I fantasize about our meeting again, now.

But in my fantasies we are nineteen and her skin is the same and *each of us beautiful* and we can spend wonderful long hours writhing on a mattress on the floor, next to radiators, making love.

She wears a corset now, of course, or should, and has cosmetics on her skin, and doubtlessly is touching up her hair, and surely uses a perfume that smells like a compost pile after a rain.

Dear old friend.

May 9

Dear Mark Edwards:

I am a "business girl." In fact, I run a travel agency.

I do not like seeing, as in one of your recent columns, prostitutes referred to as "business girls."

Are business *men* prostitutes?

A Business Girl
(Ruth Chung)

May 11

Dear Ms. Chung:
 Sure. Most of them.

Love Never Faileth,
Mark Edwards

May 8

Dear Mark Edwards:
 My parents were mean, cruel, vicious, egocentric, selfish people, and although I am almost thirty (I have a child of my own), I cannot forgive them.
 I've been working with a psychiatrist, mainly on this problem, for almost four years.
 What I'm worried about is what kind of a mother I am, after all this, and how fairly I'm treating my child.
 Often I see myself doing and hear myself saying things to my child that I just hated—and still hate!—things my parents did and said to me.

Dubious Daughter
(Barbara Horch)

May 11

Dear Mrs. Horch:
 Why don't you grow up?
 Your letter referred to yourself both as a daughter and as a parent.
 Yet I notice you signed your letter as a daughter—as a *dubious* daughter.
 Your trouble is that you'd still rather think of yourself as a daughter than as a mother.
 Accept the reality of what is: you're a Mommy, babe; you're the one who has to pick the diapers up off the floor now. Try to do it with a smile.
 Look forward, not past.

Love Never Faileth,
Mark Edwards

May 10

Dear Mark Edwards:

We think of ourselves very much as a modern couple (we invariably have wine with dinner) and lately my husband has gotten very much into group sex.

It usually gets going about four o'clock Saturday afternoon, at one person's house or another's, and I always get ready, I mean, I take a bath and so forth, but every time so far I've gotten cold feet and backed out at the last moment.

Jimmy always says the same thing when I begin saying I'm not going. He says, "You want to know you've lived."

He always goes along by himself and he always says that without me there he always feels like a fifth wheel.

Trouble is, it's ruining my weekends, too. All they run on television Saturday nights is programs for children.

Jimmy says he thinks I back out because I don't trust our friends.

Of course I do. What are friends for?

Mark, I think it's because I don't trust myself. What could I be afraid of?

Party-Pooper
(Bibs Dexter)

May 12

Dear Mrs. Dexter:

"You want to know you've lived" is the slogan of every decadent generation that has ever existed—every generation that, because of war, depression, famine, or pestilence, hasn't had to struggle simply "to live."

You have every right to think twice before you take a step toward decadence.

Maybe what you're afraid to find out about yourself is that, like every other human being, you have a proclivity toward decadence.

Love Never Faileth,
Mark Edwards

Dear Mark Edwards:

Back when I was young, I was married for a short time.

Of course I've been married since—for years and years.

For some reason, I've never told my husband or my children (who are nearly grown) about this early marriage.

I don't feel guilt about it, or anger, or bitter, or ashamed—or even particularly secretive! (Should I make the joke that somehow it never came up in conversation? Or, no one's ever asked me if I was married before?)

Now I realize how hard it would be to spring this fact on them—how much explaining I'd have to do, when, frankly, I have nothing to say!

But when I find myself thinking of this earlier marriage in front of my husband or children, I feel rather odd—as if I've been dishonest, somehow.

Two-Timer

Dear Two-Timer:

Maybe in not telling your husband and children about your previous marriage, you're simply exercising your right of privacy.

If it doesn't affect their lives in any way, and after all these years you'd now feel uncomfortable about telling them, why do they need to know?

Dear Mark Edwards:

I'm a girl in business (I run a travel agency) and I do not like seeing prostitutes referred to as "business girls."

A Business Girl

Dear Business Girl:

I may be wrong, but I believe the term "business girl" originally emerged as a joke. Women who sexually solicited men in bars were called "bar girls" (as opposed to barmaids, who actually worked in the bar, serving drinks). Thus they were called "B-girls." Although they usually had to pay off the owner of the bar in one way or another, their business was separate from the bar itself. Thus emerged the term "business girls."

In these enlightened days of greatly increased frankness, there appears to be great anxiety about how one refers to a prostitute.

A whore is a whore.

Dear Mark Edwards:

Lately my husband has gotten very much into group sex, and of course he always wants me to join in the fun, but at the last moment I always get cold feet.

He says, "You want to know you've lived."

He goes along by himself on Saturdays and he says without me there he always feels like a fifth wheel.

Trouble is, it's ruining my weekends, too.

All they run on television Saturday nights is programs for children.

Party-Pooper

Dear Party-Pooper:

Are you complaining about your husband or Saturday night television?

I've talked with the program directors of the three major networks, explaining your problem to them in detail, and they've promised to try to provide more adult programs for you Saturday nights.

Dear Mark Edwards:

My parents were mean and selfish, and although I am almost 30, I still cannot forgive them.

What I'm worried about is what kind of a mother I am, after all this, and how fairly I'm treating my child.

Dubious

Dear Dubious:

If you're almost 30, you'd better hurry up.

You have only until age 30 to learn to forgive your parents.

After age 30, you have to learn to forgive yourself.

May 13

Dear ME:

So why have I never told my wives and children about my "early marriage"?

(I not only write my column—I read it.)

(So far I've discovered that being syndicated means being a victim of typographical errors coast to coast!)

(Why did I sign that letter "Two-Timer"?)

I don't feel guilt about it, or anger, or bitterness, or shame. (Please note, with appreciation, the grammatical errors I slip into my columns—even into letters I write myself—to make them seem more authentic. [See today's column.] Who says this isn't a tough job?)

I have not told Merriam, Shelley, Mark, or Pamela about my "little marriage" with Mari.

Why not?
Because it really didn't exist.
It really didn't happen.
It happened, if at all, as a fantasy.

8.

May 13

Dear Mark Edwards:
   I have a sex problem—YOU, ya bastard.
   Every whore in this fuckin' city's on strike.
   Whaddaya want me to do—get married?

Beer-Belly Bob
(Stuart Pomeroy)

May 19

Dear Stuart "Beer-Belly Bob" Pomeroy:
   Thank you for your letter to the Mark Edwards column. Time
does not permit a personal answer.

Sincerely,
Mark Edwards

Dear Mark Edwards:

I never thought that thirty-two-year-old women have day dreams, especially recurring day dreams—I never knew there were such things as recurring day dreams—but I seem to be having some such thing, only it's not precisely a day dream because mostly I have it at night, just as I'm going to sleep, and sometimes it continues into my dreams and becomes a night dream, if you know what I mean, a situation, a sensation, a sort of mood or feeling that goes into sleep with me. And it does recur. In fact, I'm having it continually.

I'm having it so often it seems to be taking over part of my day.

I find myself thinking about it, returning to this situation, sensation, mood, feeling, whatever it is, at the oddest moments!

It goes like this:

I'm walking along Fifth Avenue in a tailored dark blue suit (I have a dark blue suit, but it's not really tailored), white blouse and gold necklace and bracelets (I have a gold necklace and bracelets, but they're only costume jewelry), swinging my handbag happily as I walk.

Ahead of me there are two black men, dressed in dark suits and hats, yellow ties, leaning against the hood of a large, dark car—an Oldsmobile, I think, or maybe a Buick.

And as I come along, they nudge each other and approach me.

"Get in the car," one of them says.

The other one opens the back seat of the car.

"Get in the car, or I'll cut you."

So I get in the back seat with one of them.

The other one begins to drive us north, and I see we're headed for Harlem!

Partway there, the man in the back seat says to me, "Why did you do it?"

"Why did I do what?"

He rolls his eyes at me and shrugs and doesn't say any more.

In Harlem, the car pulls into an alley and stops and they make me get out.

They bring me into a building, into a room, a sort of dirty old basement-type room, where there are lots of black people, mostly men, some of them sitting around a rough, wooden table.

After looking at me a long moment, one of the men says, "Take her clothes off."

So three of them strip me down, right down to my bare white skin, take off everything, while I struggle.

I say, "No, no."

Then I'm made to stand there, naked, while they all look at me. A man each side of me holds me by the wrist.

Finally, the man at the table says, "Why did you do it?"

And I say, "No, no, I didn't do it! Not even my family did it! They were machinists, from Poland. They worked in the factories, in Rochester!"

The man shakes his head up and down, slowly, and says, "You did it, too."

There's a grumbling from the other people in the room.

They begin to shout, "Take her! Take her!"

They're all shouting together.

And, quietly, the man at the table says, "Take her."

So they take me back out to the alley, dragging me by the wrists, I'm naked, but the car is gone!

Instead, there is an old, wooden, two-wheeled wagon there, with a horse or a donkey or a mule or something in front of it. You know, one of those old wagons with a waist-high railing around it, held up by spindly sticks? On its floor is hay mixed in with manure.

They pull me, push me up into the wagon, and another man comes along with chains, and while I struggle, they chain my left wrist and left ankle to the left side of the cart and my right wrist and right ankle to the right side of the cart.

All the people have come out of the building, and they are watching.

"No, no," I say.

They finish chaining me to the wagon.

A man goes to the head of the horse and picks up the lead and gives it a pull and, with the people from the building following us, we clop out of the alley into a main street in Harlem!

All the people line the sidewalks, all of them black, and other people lean out of the windows of the tenements, all of them staring at me in my white nakedness, except some of them who lower their eyes in shame for me, and most of them are silent, staring, watching me go by.

I have never felt so white in my life!

The horse in front of me relieves itself and the people behind me pick up the dung in handfuls and fling it at me. It sticks against my skin and clings to my hair.

So mortified, I struggle against my chains, thrash around in the cart.

We turn a corner, and they continue to drag me, white and naked, in chains, through the streets of Harlem, for all the people to see.

I know I'm being taken somewhere, for some purpose, but in the dream I never know where, or why.

Don't you think this is an unusual day dream for a teacher of the fifth grade?

Odd thing is, this situation, this sensation, this mood, as I say, now continues more and more during the daytime.

Here I am, doing fractions and ratio with my class, and I feel myself being dragged through Harlem naked in a wagon. We're studying the geography of Australia and I realize I'm holding my arms tight, straining against the invisible chains. We're reading *Wind in the Willows* and I envision all those black faces staring at my nakedness. While teaching my class about the Stamp Act, I feel the hay and the manure between my toes.

I call this a recurring day dream which continues into my sleep.

I wonder if it's what other people might call a fantasy?

Troubled Day-Dreamer
(Ms. Inez Oronsky)

May 19

Dear Ms. Inez (Troubled Day-Dreamer) Oronsky:

Thank you for your letter to the Mark Edwards column. Time does not permit a personal answer.

Sincerely,
Mark Edwards

May 15

Dear Mark Edwards:

I thought you might be interested in printing my recipe for shrunken heads.

First, as with all other cooking, the shopping, getting the right materials to start with, is most important.

You should expect to devote several days to your search for the right-sized head.

It is recommended you limit your search to your own town or neighborhood, as finding the right-sized head may take days of walking and, of course, you must remember that you will have the problem of disposing of the rest of the corpse. Carrying a headless corpse is cumbersome, and drippy.

Ideally, you should have the head of a reasonably small person. Experience has shown that the heads of people four feet eight or ten inches tall look best shrunken, although you can accept the heads of people up to five feet four inches tall. (There are exceptions to this, of course. Some small people have very large heads and there are tall people with small heads ideally suited to shrinking.)

Once you have spotted an acceptable head, you have the problem of arranging a moment of privacy with the person wearing the head, so you may remove it. Obviously, it is easier to get a person alone if you are his friend. If not friendly with your head, ambushing him (preferably outdoors, after dark) requires only a little forethought and good planning.

No method for severing a head (except for the guillotine) beats one firm, sideways slash at the neck with a sharp, heavy sword. It is best to remove your head from a live person (rather than killing the person first and then hacking the head off) as you will discover the blood drains from the head more easily if the head is surprised.

Too, a head surprised at being severed from its body is apt to wear a much nicer facial expression. Although originally a grimace, the process of shrinking will cause the grimace to appear more and more as a grin.

You may dispose of the rest of the body in any way convenient to you. There is little or no use for arms, legs, whatever, as leftovers.

You must do two things before you fillet the head.

First, you must remove the teeth, especially the back teeth, upper and lowers. No implement is better for this task than an ordinary pair of household pliers. If you wish, you may leave one or two upper front teeth in the gum, for decoration.

Second, turning the head upside down and entering through the neck, scoop out of the head the remaining blood, tissue, other soft matter with an ordinary tablespoon.

Allow to dry.

A certain loss of hair is to be expected but, as doubtlessly you want some hair remaining on the head, for garnish, handle the hair as carefully as possible.

Filleting the head is an arduous task, which requires both concentration and caution.

Again using a pair of ordinary pliers, reach in through the neck, grab hold of the nearest bone and break it with a quick snap of your wrist. Remove bone fragments as they become free.

WARNING: Under no circumstances—however great the temptation—use a chisel and/or screwdriver and hammer to break bone in the interior of the head. Doing so will rip the exterior skin of the head. Scars caused will prohibit uniform wrinkling of the head. Such traumas to the head will cause a mess and oblige you to start all over again.

Immediately bones are removed from the head, fill head with hot, wet sand. Do not pack too tightly. Obviously, head must be kept upside down while filled with sand, to prevent leakage through the nose and ears.

Allow to steep for two or three days. As the sand cools and dries, the head will begin to shrink.

Once thoroughly dry, proceed to remove five tbsps sand a day from head, until sand is completely gone. This will permit uniform shrinkage and wrinkling.

A properly shrunken head is no more than eight cm long, and five cm wide.

Sincerely,
Julia Guile
(Mrs. Lewis Delp)

May 19

Dear "Julia Guile"—Mrs. Lewis Delp:

Thank you for your letter to the Mark Edwards column. Time does not permit a personal answer.

Sincerely,
Mark Edwards

May 17

Dear Mark Edwards:

I would like to know what is the personal effect upon you of writing the "Dear Mark Edwards" column.

Sincerely,
Dr. Frank Miller

May 19

Dear Dr. "Frank" Miller:

Thank you for your letter to the Mark Edwards column. Time does not permit a personal answer.

Sincerely,
Mark Edwards

May 16

Dear Mark Edwards:

Not all us street walkers are "women," "ladies," "girls" at all—although some of us would like to be.

The Boys of the Night
(Troy Willard)

May 19

Dear Troy "Boys of the Night" Willard:

Thank you for your letter to the Mark Edwards column. Time does not permit a personal answer.

Sincerely,
Mark Edwards

May 17

Dear Mark Edwards:

I am eighteen (no longer "jail bait"!), red-haired, beautiful, and read your column every day and want you right now (or any time in the future) to come fuck fuck fuck me.

Address above. During the daytime, I'm usually out back—by the pool.

Welcoming Bod
(Mary Knorr)

May 19

Dear Mary ("Welcoming Bod") Knorr:
Thank you for your letter to the Mark Edwards column. Time does not permit a personal answer.

Sincerely,
Mark Edwards

May 17

Dear Mark Edwards:
If I am sitting in my basement room, my "rec room," thinking, over and over, what I'm thinking, it stands to reason that a great many other people in this nation, maybe this world, are sitting in their rec rooms thinking the same things.

I talk to my wife about it, and she shrugs and says, "Yes, dear."

Somehow I don't dare talk to my friends about it, the other men in my law firm, even the guys I play golf with. I guess I'm afraid it would sound weak-sisterish, mealy-mouthed. But I swear I see it in their eyes, in their attitudes. I swear they don't dare talk to me about it either.

It would be interesting to me if you printed something like this letter in your column and see if anyone else writes in and says, "I know what that guy's talking about."

The way I define it, we were (at least I was) brought up in a goal-oriented society. Always had to have a goal. Always had to be reaching for it. Didn't matter too much (except *really*) if you ever achieved your goal, as long as you had one and were reaching for it.

The goals are gone. They have disappeared from our society. Evaporated.

Or, somehow as I was becoming middle-aged, Society's goals shifted, became something I don't understand, something that doesn't relate to my youth, something I don't recognize, something meaningless to me.

Now, I'm not so big a fool that I think now, or ever did

think, the goals I was brought up on were so great. I remember too well what they were.

Absolutely materialistic.

The big house on lots of land, clipped lawn. People clipping your lawn for you, goddamn it, who showed some respect when you went out to get into your big car and evidenced a kindly interest in how *they* were doing with *your* roses. A Cadillac, a Lincoln—maybe a good-looking, twelve-cylinder car, that some-one else kept clean for you. At *least* a car you could get into the back seat of without having to transform yourself into a bag of potatoes! At *least* a car big enough for you to drive without having to take your hat off because there simply isn't room for it between the top of your head and the roof!

I know the goals were materialistic. Someone to get you a cup of coffee when you went into the office in the morning. A quiet club where you could have lunch with your friends, and maybe a drink after work. Going to play golf on Saturday or Sunday without having to beat away loud women and shrieking children with your number four iron!

Now, I'm not the only one in this world who went to work in a grocery store at age sixteen to earn money for a college tuition, waited on tables all through college, got myself into law school, worked like a bastard, winter and summer, to pay my own bills, got myself into a half-decent law firm where I put in thirty years to become a partner—while taking three years out of my life to sweat it out in a stinking tin battleship in the Indian Ocean.

But a lot of fellows didn't do this. Most of the fellows I grew up with fucked around and drank beer and went to ball games. Anyone would have liked to do that. I would have liked to have done that.

I had goals. I was goal-oriented.

Where's the difference between the way they live right now and the way I live? Where's my reward?

Yes, I live in a house in the suburbs. It is mostly basement. Surrounded by cement blocks, a furnace, washer, dryer, pine paneling, and windows too high to see out of. Have you noticed that almost all Americans seem to be living in their own basements? We've gone underground, as a people. A fact,

I'm sure, which will be of great interest to future anthropologists.

Instead of having land I have what is called *a lot*—which is *a little*. Measured in square feet instead of acres. Which I mow myself on Saturdays and Sundays because the golf course is so full, so jam-packed with people running back and forth exclaiming over each other's clothing fashions that teeing off, actually hitting the ball, takes on the aspect of a public act of violence!

I certainly can't ask anyone at the office to get me a cup of coffee without clearly offending the femininity, or masculinity, of everyone in sight.

I have to wait my turn at a lunch counter.

Yes, I have assets of over three hundred thousand dollars. Yes, my wife and I spent a month in Europe six years ago.

So what?

What does it all matter in my daily life, my way of life?

Why didn't I fuck around and drink beer and go to the ball games? My way of life wouldn't be much different if I had done so.

You know, I feel rather stupid. I seem to have made a poorer bargain than did those people I used to consider idiots and fools.

What happened to the so-called American "good life"?

Why did I believe in it, work for it?

Who robbed me of it?

Mr. What Happened?
(James C. Maurer, Esq.)

May 19

Dear Mr. James C. (Mr. What Happened?) Maurer:

Thank you for your letter to the Mark Edwards column. Time does not permit a personal answer.

Sincerely,
Mark Edwards

May 19

Dear ME:

If things are going badly, all you need is an assistant to make things go worse.

A assistant.

Monroe Lipton, publisher, gave me a new office and News/ Features Syndicate gave me *a* assistant.

At this writing, I doubt I'll ever get used to either of them.

Everything in the office is cockeyed: the desk angled so that it looks like it's about to make a dash through the door; the type-writer in a corner as if it had just read one of our columns and wishes to hide its blushing keyboard from the world; the drawers of the filing cabinet agape, boxes everywhere, full of I don't know what.

Ms. Halamay is also full of I don't know what.

If she had been put together by an artist more detached than herself, doubtlessly she would be entitled *An Arrangement in Black and White.*

Black shoes. White legs. Longish black skirt. White blouse. Black coral necklace. White face. Black horn-rimmed glasses. White forehead stretched so tight by black hair either side pulled to a bun in back her whole face would have to remain expressionless even if confronted by a salivating bear with the pox.

Gently, I had fiddled around my new office expressing, to my new assistant, mild discomfort at the mess.

Then I found the postal cards. A stack of them, on my desk.

Ordinary postal cards with a message printed on back which I first read in curiosity, second in astonishment, third in fury.

"What the hell is this?" I exclaimed.

Ms. Halamay was picking up a box and putting it down again. For all I had been able to see, she had been picking up and putting down the same damned box all morning.

"What—" I exclaimed more loudly. "The hell—" I choked. "Is this?"

Ms. Halamay, clearly never trained to be responsive to choked exclamations, said, "Ummm?"

"This card, Ms. Halamay. This postcard. This postcard with the printing on back. My God, Ms. Halamay."

"Yes."

She smiled, as if to say that was that.

I read the postal card in as steady a voice as I could muster.

" 'Thank you for your letter to the Mark Edwards column. Time

does not permit a personal answer. Sincerely, Mark Edwards'!
Ms. Halamay!" I roared.

There were stacks of these cards on the desk. Thousands of
them.

"Ms. Halamay!" I said.

"Yes," she said conclusively.

"No," I said. "No! No! No!"

Box in hand, she might have raised her eyebrows a millimeter.
Then again, her bun in back may have given her a twinge.

"God! You haven't sent any of these out, have you?"

"They're your new correspondence cards," she said.

"You haven't sent any of these out?"

"Of course."

"To people?"

"To your correspondents."

"Oh, God, no. You've sent these out? You've actually sent these
out to human beings?"

"They're standard." She lifted the box again.

"They're inhuman!"

"They're recommended by the Syndicate."

" 'Thank you for your letter to the Mark Edwards column'?
'Time does not permit a personal answer'? 'Sincerely, Mark Edwards'? That's recommended?"

"What else are you going to do?"

"Answer the damned letters!"

"You can't answer the letters, Mr. Edwards."

"I can. I will. I always have."

"Yes. I know. I've been through your files. Very unwise of
you."

"Unwise?"

She nodded at the box she had just put down. "Doubles your
chances of lawsuits. Especially the way you answer them."

"Ms. Halamay. These are human beings who write to me.
Most of them, anyway. Most of the letters are sincere. Haven't
you read them?"

"Oh, yes indeed."

"They're confidential. Get the point? That's why we publish
the letters under phony names. So people will feel free to write
in what they want."

"Listen, Mr. Edwards, if you would read the postcard closely, you will see above your name the word 'Sincerely.' That means you are answering their letters *sincerely*."

"Do you know what the word *sincere* means?"

"Without wax," she said. "*Sine cere*."

"These postcards blow the confidentiality of the whole operation. You're violating the privacy of the people who write to me. You send them one of these open postcards and everyone in the neighborhood knows the person has written me—even knows the phony name the person has used." By then I had found a stack of addressed cards, ready to mail. "Their mailman, their husbands, their wives, their children, their sisters, their cousins, their uncles, and their aunts!"

"Gilbert and Sullivan."

"Them, too!"

"Mr. Edwards, I was sent down from Chicago—"

"If I answer the letters, personally, a personal letter in a sealed envelope—"

"To shape this operation up—"

"I can write anything I want, maybe even be a help to them—whaddaya mean, 'shape this operation up'?"

"And I intend to do it."

She put down the box again. I hadn't seen her pick it up. She was getting pretty good at it.

"Absolutely inhuman!" I said. "What do you think this column is fighting?"

She looked at me. There may have been genuine curiosity in her face. She did not know what my column was fighting. Anyway, she looked at me.

"We're fighting the inhuman. The impersonal. The bureaucratic . . ."

I stopped, because she seemed visibly disappointed in my answer as to what we were fighting.

She picked up the box again.

"Mr. Edwards, this column is now a lot bigger than you realize. Which is why I was sent here to help you."

"Then help me answer the goddamned letters."

"We cannot answer the letters, except for a postcard acknowledging receipt."

"I can. You can. We all can."

"You'd need a staff of one thousand organized psychiatrists, ministers, social workers, and orthopedists—"

"We'll get 'em."

"We'll not get them. The Syndicate will not get them! Not pay for them!"

"Ms. Halamay, you speak of the 'Syndicate' as if it were something with a bulge under its jacket and garlic on its breath."

"It's a business."

"'Business,'" I scoffed. "'Business' is an excuse for everything that happens in this country."

"Furthermore," she said, putting down the box again. She seemed to be putting the box down more than she was picking it up. "Do you think someone who writes in a recipe for shrunken heads deserves an answer?"

"Shrunken heads?"

"Shrunken heads."

"I didn't read that letter. Sounds amusing. Are we going to use it in the column?"

"No."

"Why not?"

"Too stupid."

"Ms. Halamay." I began tearing up the postal cards, addressed ones first. "The Syndicate may have sent you here to assist me, but it's my column—"

She pointed to three canvas U.S. Mail sacks in the corner. "You think you can answer all these letters? The mailroom is sending up two more sacks!"

"It's better not to answer them at all."

"It's Syndicate policy!"

"Not my policy. I never insult anyone unless I intend to." I was getting tired of tearing up postal cards but felt I couldn't leave the job for my assistant to finish. "If you ever send one of these postcards again—or anything like them—if I ever see or hear of these postcards again—"

"The Syndicate hired me," she said with the certainty of someone who was there at the time, "and you can't fire me."

"No," I said. "But consider this . . . I was trying to think up something she might consider. A threat. Something that would absolutely devastate her. Make her self-image quake in its imaginary boots. "I can," I said, finally, "have your legs painted red, your arms yellow, your neck blue, and your face green. Consider that."

She looked properly horrified.

Sometimes it's well to let people know they're dealing with somewhat of a madman.

She continued to stare at me silently while I finished tearing up the *Sincerely, Mark Edwards* postal cards.

"I'm going away for the weekend," I said. "To cheer on my daughter's school, Rounds School, while trouncing St. Axelrood's at the wonderful, healthy American sport of baseball. I will be the loudly cheering parent somewhere along the first base line. No phone calls, please. No telegrams. And especially," I said while annihilating the last of them, "no postcards."

Oh, my! Oh, me! What complaint have the Fates against me that they do so persistently surround me with women like Ms. Halamay?

9.

May 20

Dear ME:

Oh, my God.

It is midnight, Saturday, and I am where I least expected to be, in my bleak new office, desk askew, typewriter shamefaced in the corner, filing cabinets agape, boxes everywhere resting from Ms. Halamay's uplifting.

I am not entirely in order myself.

Pamela thinks I am enjoying the weekend at Shelley's school. I suppose Shelley thinks I've gone home to Pamela.

I am neither place, and have enjoyed nothing.

I have the growing impression I have spent at least part of this weekend on some other planet in some other galaxy, where the denizens communicate with quick looks, birdlike tosses of the head, guttural monosyllables, and apelike shrugs.

I was at an American school.

Dear Daddy Dodderer drove onto the campus of Rounds School, waving, with aplomb, I thought, at the campus cop at the gate, otherwise not stopping to interview him, through a jungle of darting, bare-legged wildlife (teen-aged boys and girls, I think), honking away those on bikes who threatened my fenders, pulling up in front of Shelley's dormitory building with, I thought, the correct dignity of someone my age and distinction about to be warmly greeted.

Getting out of the car, I noticed my arrival was creating quite a stir among the wildlife. My transport and I were surrounded by curious, chattering jungle forms, some straddling bikes, some carrying tennis rackets, one carrying a formidable lacrosse stick. Heads hung from the windows.

From a distance came the banshee wailing of a siren.

Of course at that time I had not been informed of local customs, had not been told that only the cars of visiting heads of state, visiting poets, and alumni over eighty were allowed on campus.

"Oh, my God!" I heard a familiar voice, from above, call out over the din.

There was a loud clattering from the building's interior stairs and Shelley appeared, a huge boy (six feet two, with the face of a seven-year-old; he looked like an uncut custard pie on stilts) at her heels. She looked frightened beyond belief.

"Shelley, old girl," I said, preparatory to bussing her one.

"Dad! You're not supposed to be on campus!"

"That's all right. Nothing he sees or hears will shock your old Dad."

I had decided that—as a matter of policy—on the way up.

"I mean, the car's not supposed to be on campus."

"Oh." A minor infraction, I thought, in a badly shattered social environment. "I have something for you in the trunk."

The huge boy behind her had tossed his head several times already, whether in an effort to quell the chattering natives or as a nervous tick I couldn't fathom.

"Is that your car?" Shelley asked. "What the hell is it, anyway?"

"A Bentley."

"What's a Bentley?"

"A Rolls-Royce," I said loudly enough for all the curious audience—even the back rows—to hear, "with a nose job."

She stuck a bare toe against a tire. It did not penetrate.

Shelley and the huge boy were wearing matching torn blue-jean shorts and T-shirts. If the tears didn't match precisely, at least they complemented each other. Anatomically, as Merriam might point out.

"Is this Antoinette?" I put my hand out to the large object, who took it. "How's your elbow?"

"Elbow?"

"This is Nicky," Shelley said.

"Oh? What happened to Tony?"

Shelley said, "Tony plays second base," exactly as if she were properly answering the question.

The siren was getting louder. Or closer, I should say. As it was on a police car. Which was approaching.

"Do you play baseball?" I asked Nicky.

"Pitch."

"I can't hear you. There's a siren . . ."

"I pitch."

"I see."

"The car, Dad."

A hot-looking policeman got out of the hot-looking police car, slamming the door with such ire one would think he had just heard for the first time that crime pays.

"This your car, Mister?"

"It's a Bentley."

"It's an obscene car, Dad."

"Gross," added a kid on a yellow twelve-speed bike.

"Obscene? Gross?"

"What are you," yelled a kid from one of the back rows, "some kind of a nut drive a car like that?"

"Hey, Mister," yelled a voice above a pair of legs dangling from the branch of a nearby tree. "How many miles do you get to the fluid ounce?"

"I rented it," I whispered to Shelley. "It's a rented car."

Relief washed her face. "It's a rented car!" she declaimed three times, north, then east, then south.

"What the hell do you mean by bringing the car on campus?" the policeman asked.

"I didn't know I wasn't supposed to."

"You didn't see the signs?"

"I didn't see the signs."

"You didn't see the officer at the gate?"

"I saw the officer at the gate."

"You think he stands there eight hours just to attract bugs?"

"Officer, I have something for my daughter in the trunk. Some Coke . . ."

The wildlife began muttering, tossing heads, twitching.

The pie-faced boy on stilts, eyes sliding sideways, took five paces backward.

Shelley said, "Oh, no."

"Unreal," the cop said. "Who is this guy?"

"This *guy*"? Mark Edwards in a Bentley? "This *guy*"?

"Shelley," whispered I, "will you please tell him—them—I'm your father, I pay some of the bills around here, I'm Mark Edwards of News slash Features Syndicate? . . ."

"No."

"Open your trunk, Mister."

". . . And that because of the nature of my work—being a syndicated columnist—I am the most understanding, *au courant* of all doddering daddies?"

"No."

"Open your trunk, Mister."

"I was about to."

I showed him the case of Coca-Cola.

"It was cold when I bought it," I said, trying to hand him one.

Instead of taking it, he put his hand to his face, and said, "Unreal."

Shelley had sat down on the dormitory steps.

Nicky Pie-face took one step forward.

More for something to do than anything else, I lifted the case of Coke out of the trunk and handed it to Nicky.

Unexpectedly, for such a large boy, he was shaking.

"I'll just duck upstairs for a minute, see my daughter's room, then I'll move the car, Officer. Sorry for the trouble."

The chattering, giggling wildlife surrounded a sylvan pool of silence—Shelley, Nicky, and the cop.

I entered the building.

Shelley and Nicky caught up with me halfway up the stairs.

Her/their room: bed frames, springs, neatly stored in one corner, leaning against the wall; underclothes, sweat socks, sneakers, a jockstrap, a sweater, jeans on the floor; two desks side by side (on one a bottle of bourbon and a baseball glove, which shows some respect); two mattresses side by side on the floor, crumpled sheets.

"Ah!" I said. "Looks like a *Good Housekeeping* layout. 'How Young America Lives.'"

I was trying to find a large poster on the wall, of five nude twenty-year-olds, both sexes, two electric guitars, attractive.

I failed.

"How's old Candy?" I asked.

"Gandy."

"How's old Gandy?" I asked.

"She had to go home this weekend," Shelley answered. "Abortion."

"Oh. I'll bet her parents are glad to see her."

"How's that woman you live with?"

"Sends her best. Had to stay home this weekend and tear someone's movie to ribbons."

Nicky had put the case of Coke, dripping, on one of the desks.

"The cop is blowing your horn," he said. "I think he wants your car moved."

"You have that impression?"

Shelley handed me the bottle of bourbon.

"How nice of you," I said. "Can you two have lunch with me?"

"No," Nicky said.

"He has lots to do," Shelley said. "Sit in a sauna, put his pitching arm in a whirlpool—"

"Pressures, pressures," I clucked. "What about you, Shelley?"

"I have to work in the box office."

"Box office?"

"For the game."

"You're selling tickets to parents who support the school?"

"Of course."

I said, "Of course. Neither of you can have lunch with me?" The policeman was blowing the Bentley's horn with increasing frequency. No wonder they didn't allow cars on campus. They were apt to become very noisy. "Well, then, I'll bang off to the hotel. . . ."

I wished Nicky luck at pitching, told him I'd be rooting for him, wished Shelley luck at selling tickets, went downstairs, freed the cop for other duties, drove off campus, waving, again with aplomb, I thought, at the cop at the gate, found the motel, checked in, went to my room, and discovered it was only eleven o'clock. The game wasn't until two. I had plenty of time, I noticed. To have lunch. Alone. While Shelley watched Nicky's pitching arm submerged in a whirlpool.

I took a long, hot shower, and that only took three and a half minutes.

I thought it would be nice to have a drink before lunch.

It was nice.

It was also not quite eleven-thirty when I finished it.

So I had another, which was also nice.

It was also only ten minutes to twelve when I had finished it.

The dining room, even in a motel, wouldn't open for lunch until at least twelve. And who wanted to be the first one in a dining room, especially when eating alone?

My third drink stimulated thought. Or an incipient rage. Or something.

Until then, I had been musing how nice it had been to drive the Bentley.

That Shelley had been ashamed by the Bentley crept in first as a suspicion, and then as a certainty.

Curious, I philosophized, how the rules of Society change. Children may enjoy total sexual intimacy, an abortion is accepted as just something to do on a weekend, but it is simply awful of Daddy to drive a large car onto campus.

My memory's eyes wandered over Shelley's room. The jockstrap on the floor. The poster of five nudes on the wall. The baseball glove on the desk. The mattresses shoved together on the floor.

The morals of a mongoose and the intellectual potential of a sleeping rattlesnake.

Pamela certainly can turn a phrase.

Sometime then, just before I was to take myself to lunch, still reviewing the scene of my arrival—Shelley suddenly sitting down on the steps, Nicky Pie-face suddenly taking a few steps backward, the cop saying "Unreal"—the ultimate realization hit me.

Coke. Coca-Cola.

Cocaine!

Any chance of your smuggling some coke over the state border for us?

Of course I'll sneak Coke across the state border to you. Is it more expensive there? Wouldn't you rather have a case of fruit juice?

YEEEEEEEEEE!

That's all right. Nothing he sees or hears will shock your old Dad.

Those kids, those children, expected me to supply them with cocaine!

Because of the nature of my work—being a syndicated columnist—I am the most understanding, au courant of all doddering daddies.

And they believe it!

Shocked, stewing, enraged about cocaine, I tapped myself with another bourbon.

Shocked, stewing, enraged about cocaine, I missed lunch.

Shocked, stewing, enraged about cocaine, time passed.

I didn't get to the baseball game until the second inning.

Shelley had a nice seat for me near the Rounds School bench.

Both teams were wearing shorts.

Not very traditional, but at least the children still like the game of baseball. Between fucks and sniffs of coke.

St. Axelrood's, 1

Rounds School, 0

Nicky Pie-face, the current adventurer in my daughter's pants, was pitching.

I assumed Tony, the past adventurer in my daughter's pants, was the big pimple on second.

Shelley, of course, was deeply in conversation with a boy in the St. Axelrood's uniform, swinging a bat.

A future adventurer in my daughter's pants?

Nicky was a beautiful pitcher.

I figured he had been put on the mound after Rounds School had lost the run in the first inning.

With those long arms and legs, his windup was slow, covered a large territory, controlled, hard to detect. His aim was nearly perfect.

By the end of the third inning, I saw he was a masterful psychologist of the mound.

Twice, to apparently good batters, his first pitch had been a slow, wide, wobbly ball. Then two perfect strikes fired in rapid succession. A high, stupid-looking ball. A low, fast perfect strike.

For two other batters, he zipped two along the outside, drawing them into the box, then served up his third strike fast on the near side of the box.

He gave away nothing.

I had never thought a fifteen-year-old boy—even with a pie-face on top of stilts—could be such a beautiful pitcher.

At the top of the fifth, Nick, arms gangling at his side, ambled over to me saying, "How am I doin', Mr. Edwards?"

Which is when I stood up and clipped him on the jaw.

All of him fell down.

As Buzz Hodd, or some other inferior sportswriter might write, the fans went wild.

Gasps of dismay.

Cries of outrage.

Other exclamations.

It occurred to me in a flash it would be very well for me to find my car, get in it, and put a state border between me and the baseball diamond at Rounds School.

I certainly didn't want to be called as a witness to this incident!

So I drove back to the city, turned the car in to the garage from which I had rented it (assuring them I certainly would never rent a Bentley again!), and taxied to the office.

Where I didn't expect to be.

Two o'clock Sunday morning.

Now I suppose I'll get some silly letter from Shelley.

Or worse, hear nothing from her.

My God, it's awfully hard to know how to handle children!

May 19

Dear Mark Edwards:
You're playing God without a license.

Catcher-In-The-Rye
(Stan Milan)

May 22

Dear Mr. Milan:
So are you.

Love Never Faileth,
Mark Edwards

May 20

Dear Mark Edwards:
I doubt I'll send this letter—even for the comfort of having written it.

Never having thought about such things before, I suppose your newspaper column fulfills a kind of socially useful function. Maybe all of us, at one time or another, suffer from something we have a great need to express, but have no one to whom we may express such things safely. My talking to a psychiatrist would ruin my career. My talking to my wife would ruin our marriage. I guess I have no friends.

I am an extremely high ranked naval officer. Well, I'm an Admiral. I'm approaching my mid-fifties. Navy career all the way—since the age of seventeen.

I'm married to a wonderful gal, and we have three daughters. I guess our lives have always been sort of unsettled—moving every three years—but that's life for a military family. We have always maintained the most comfortable home we could, under whatever circumstances we were assigned. Even during my tours of sea duty (and they have been frequent) my wife has maintained a comfortable, secure home for the family, and I love her very much.

I'm in love with a young officer. What else can I say? A male. A boy. I love him. Such a thing has never happened to me before—never entered my head. I've lived a man's life—football team captain in high school, into the Naval Academy at seventeen, married the year I graduated, mostly good, active duty (I've stayed away from desk jobs as much as anyone can in this man's Navy). My great pride has been in my ability to run men—to know instinctively when to bear down on them, when to let up. I believe most of my success in the Navy has come from my talent for dealing with men.

I have never previously had a homosexual impulse in my life— consciously.

True romance: I first saw Kip (His initials are K.I.P.—everyone calls him Kip; it's part of his attraction. Maybe he wouldn't have struck me so deeply if his name were John) while I was on an inspection of a D.E. that had been at sea for three months trying out some classified equipment. It was his job to explain the results of the experiments to me (my job to pretend I understood!). First I noticed his hands: sunburned, smooth, calm, moving as if they had a life of their own. Then I noticed the veins in his face and neck, bluish beneath that tanned, smooth, unusually transparent skin. Then I began thinking about the rest of his skin. Me! Thinking of a boy this way! His hair is thick, brown, his eyes blue and surprisingly open and frank (I think he must be a little nearsighted). He had lunch with us. Not even knowing that I was doing it—conversationally—I was springing him free from the D.E. and having him transferred to Command—my office. What Admiral wants, Admiral gets.

I realized what I had done, later (even admitted to myself why I had done it), and said to myself, "Oh, so what. That's the end of that." Then I began being aware of him as he moved around my office. His eyes. His hands. His shoulders. His ass. I began including him unnecessarily in meetings in my office, for the sheer pleasure of watching him. I began having him drive me places. Once, on a hot day, we stopped along the shore and had a swim together. I brought him home to dinner, to my youngest daughter, and she confirms he's a real beautiful kid.

I think he's a man. I think he has no idea that I think of him, sitting alone in my office; at home, in bed, at night. But what if he isn't? What if he would enjoy my attentions? What if he would enjoy, even benefit from, sexual intimacy with me?

I am disgusted by myself the same time I am thrilled by

myself. All this has made me less of an officer. I find I am more hesitant, less decisive, unsure of my masculinity, wondering if I am going crazy! I figure I must either come to terms sexually with this boy, or have him shipped out to the farthest corner of the earth.

I think I will send this letter, just to see what you will say. Obviously, signing my name even "confidentially" to you would make me an instant security risk. I think you can tell from the letter it is sincere.

Sincerely,
The Not Admirable

(May 24)

Dear Mark Edwards:

I am a high-ranking military officer, middle-aged and happily married to a wife I love, with daughters I love—suddenly stuck on a boy I love!

I am not conscious of ever having had a homosexual impulse previously in my life.

I have had this young man reassigned to my office. I ask him to drive me places. Once, we stopped along the shore and went swimming together.

This situation worries me for all the obvious reasons.

Do I tell this boy about my sexual interest in him, or do I have him shipped to the farthest corner of the earth?

A Senior Officer

Dear Senior Officer:

What puzzles me in your letter is that you say this is the first homosexual impulse you've ever consciously had in your life, and yet you are so frank about it.

If this is true, what has caused you to stop suppressing your homosexual nature?

There are so many definitions of homosexuality I doubt anyone knows what the hell it is.

A man loves his sailboat and touches it lovingly. His horse. His car. His beer mug. His violin. The squash he grew in his garden. Men love men, in a million different ways, for a million different reasons.

Yet if a man touches another man lovingly, that's supposed to mean there is something perverted deep in his nature?

I suspect you're in love with the young man you once were—and have replaced him with this young man under your command.

Or maybe you're in love with the son you never had.

Enjoy love where and how and when you find it.

And I suspect, sir, if the young man is as attractive as you say, male-oriented or not, he is used to the sexual tensions around him and will be able to handle you more deftly than you expect—without ruining either your career or your marriage.

I'm sure he'd far rather be given the chance than be "shipped to the farthest corner of the earth."

Dear Mark Edwards:

You're playing God without a license.

Catcher-In-The-Rye

Dear Catcher-In-The-Rye:

So who's giving them out?

Dear Mark Edwards:

I've just discovered the son of our next-door neighbors and dear friends stole a $20 bill from my kitchen counter.

How do I handle this?

Worried

Dear Worried:

Bash him in the face until he gives the money back, then help him make up an excuse to explain his bashed-in face to his parents.

Everyone's entitled to goof a little.

May 23

Dear Dad:

Do I have your permission to transfer to St. Axelrood's School next term?

Shelley

May 25

Dear Shelley:

I think it might be wise all round for you to transfer to St. Axelrood's School next term.

I have reason to suspect St. Axelrood's beat Rounds School in the big annual baseball game last Saturday (sorry I had to leave early) and it is always well to go where the baseball is best. . . .

10.

Dear Mark Edwards:

How come the only guys on the t.v. programs who drive big cars and live in big houses are crooks and murderers?

Aren't there any good rich people?

> The Contestant
> (José Oberon)

May 28

Dear Mr. Oberon:

The people in this country who drive big cars and live in big houses are the television networks' executives, producers, stars, and sponsors.

Having themselves portrayed on television as evil is their way of keeping the masses down, making you think that, to be rich, invariably you must sacrifice your morality. This allows you to be content in your poverty.

In previous centuries the masses were told it was harder for a rich man to get into heaven than a hawser to pass through the eye of a needle.

Same difference.

This moral superiority that is provided you makes a nice gravy for your rice and beans.

Lap it up.

Love Never Faileth,
Mark Edwards

May 25

Dear ME:

This A.M., bright and early at the office.

"Good morning, Mr. Edwards."

"Good morning, Ms. Halamay."

"Frightful lot of complaint calls and telegrams regarding your advocating homosexuality in yesterday's column."

"I advocated homosexuality?"

"In your letter to 'Senior Officer.'"

"That advocated homosexuality?"

"It did."

"Oh." What had ever, truly, warmed Ms. Halamay's loins? "Love never faileth."

Slowly my office is getting better organized. Not by anybody doing anything about it. Just by things getting shoved around for convenient use.

"Ms. Halamay?"

"Yes?"

"Let's fuck."

"What?"

"Let's fuck."

"Certainly," she said. "Or would you rather a cup of tea?"

May 23
Dear Mark Edwards:
I'm considered an old lady and in truth I'm nearing eighty but who says old ladies don't have as much sexual interest in men as we ever had?
And I don't mean *old* men.
I have as much sexual interest in *old* men as I ever had—not much.
I want younger men—the same younger men I always wanted!
No Foolin'
(Mrs. Frances Heath)

May 28
Dear Mrs. Heath:
I'll be right over.

Love Never Faileth,
Mark Edwards

May 24
TO: Mark Edwards
FROM: Monroe Lipton, Publisher
I see from today's column you're still zapping them in there, Mark—recommending rape in the Navy and bashing the neighbors' kid's head in.
Did I tell you those advertisers who dropped us, because of you, are now back buying their full linage—and at a higher price?
Circulation's surveys keep indicating the readers like your column alot.

May 25
TO: Monroe Lipton, Publisher
FROM: Mark Edwards
There is no such word as "alot."

May 26

Dear Mark Edwards:

I've just discovered our public junior high school is teaching a course in sex education.

Instruction in sex education and other such matters having to do with morality definitely belong in the home.

I know this issue has been raised before, but do we have any legal standing at this point in preventing the schools from teaching our son their version of sexual morality?

Sex Preventative
(Mrs. Karl Haneman)

May 28

Dear Mrs. Haneman:

Have no fear.

Thanks to timorous, ignorant, thumb-sucking idiots like you, sex education courses in American public schools are about as useful and informative as courses in Astronomy to earthworms.

They're nothing but abstract courses in fertilization—useful only to people who plan to run honey farms at an altitude of 10,000 meters or above.

From such a course your son will learn no more about the practical mechanics of sex than he'd learn about driving a car from a course in Algebra.

Social diseases are at epidemic levels—and becoming increasingly virulent. Twenty percent of current marriages are forced. And the abortion factories are running shifts twenty-four hours a day.

All this wouldn't be happening if there were anything approaching sex education in our schools.

There can be no moral judgment or consideration, no moral choice, which is not based on an informed, educated understanding of the practical mechanics of what one is doing.

Instead of worrying about what your son might learn, why don't you worry about what he and his playmates won't learn, and get in there and work on improving these courses in sex education?

That way he may not end up as immorally stupid as you are.

Love Never Faileth,
Mark Edwards

May 24

TO: Mark Edwards
FROM: Owen Hatch
News/Features Syndicate

Please get your column in twenty-fours hours earlier.

Please also supply us with three or four extra, general columns to run in place of any our editors feel don't work out.

Today's column, including letters to "Senior Officer" and "Worried," shouldn't have run.

May 25

TO: Owen Hatch
FROM: Mark Edwards

I don't write this column.

The People do.

Currently, obscenity, etc., is defined as that which is "offensive to community standards."

Our mail comes from the Community.

Victorian advice, from me, would not be acceptable to the People.

My constantly advising them to consult their psychiatrist, gynecologist, minister, or podiatrist would make for one helluva dull column.

This is my column. Let me do it my way.

And, speaking of obscenities, thanks for sending me Ms. Halamay.

She's a prune, and you know what the effect is of prunes upon columnists.

It's the column that's supposed to run regularly—not me!

May 23

Dear Mark Edwards:

Two weeks ago, when we returned from a family camping trip, we discovered our house—our home!—had been burglarized.

Everything—our color T.V., our stereo, silverware I had from my husband's family, my husband's movie camera and projector, my son's calculator, a few pieces of jewelry my husband has bought me over the years I had hidden in a sewing bag in my closet—everything! was gone.

Now, you read about burglary all the time, and watch it on television, and our neighbors have been burglarized, but somehow this bothers me more than I thought—more than just the loss of the objects.

The thought of someone actually breaking into our house and taking our things—I don't know—it makes me very nervous, and depressed.

My husband says I'll snap out of it, but in two weeks, I haven't.

I Was Robbed!
(Mrs. Howard Kellenberg)

May 28

Dear Mrs. Kellenberg:

What you feel, having had your family home burglarized, is akin to the feeling of having been raped.

It's not just the loss you suffered that is weighing upon you, but the feeling that you have been outrageously violated—which you have been.

And this makes you feel dreadfully vulnerable, doesn't it? As if anyone could come along and violate you at any time.

Whoever did this to you should be put in boiling water up to their necks and left there until their bones melt.

But, of course, with the efficiency of the average police in this country, your burglars won't lose even a wink of sleep.

Take deep breaths and get busy. You'll get over it.

Love Never Faileth,
Mark Edwards

May 29

Dear Kids All:

(By which I mean Jason Jensen, Jr., Pamela Jensen [Jr.], Shelley Edwards, and Mark Edwards, Jr.)

Now for the big news! The big surprise!

Are yew all ready for this?

As I'm sure you're all aware, your friend and Daddy (referred to as Dear Daddy Dodderer by some particularly irreverent citizens among you) turns forty years old in this very month of July (no applause, please; a subdued "Here! Here!" will suffice). . . . And, what's more, has a new office gem, *a* assistant name of Ms. Halamay who (the big shots at News/Features Syndicate believe) can run my column well enough to allow the above-fondly-referred-to Dear Daddy Dodderer a period of time away from the office. . . .

Therefore, whereas and heretoforth, as I slip into the cocktail hour of my life, be advised I have rented a big old summer place out on the Island for the two weeks surrounding the Festive Occasion marking my ascendancy into my Fifth Decade trekking this Earth. . . .

With the hope and expectation that us Family will get together for swimming, sailing, tennis, volleyball, batting practice, whist, and, conceivably, even a good old try at choral singing!

As the Day Itself is the twenty-third of the month, I have taken the house from the fifteenth on. So . . .

Mark your calendars!
Whet your appetites!
Appear!

> Dear Daddy Dodderer
> (Mr. Mark Edwards, Sr.)

(May 29)

Dear Mark Edwards:
  You're always harping on the prostitution issue, but you haven't said all that much about women's inferior role in general.

> Hey, Now

Dear Hey, Now:
  In general, I believe women are superior.
  That's why, if they're willing to have babies and be nice, they get to stay home while men support them.

Dear Mark Edwards:
  Silva Mellon, a colleague, a while ago tried to organize us professional prostitutes and ended up knifed under a parked car.
  So we all went on strike.
  So far, we're starvin', the pimps are beatin' on us, and Silva's murder hasn't been solved.
  Any new ideas?

> Professional Prostitutes of
> America United

Dear PPAU:

You wouldn't be getting any more attention from the authorities if you were taxpayers.

But—seeing you're united—you might try marching on police head-quarters, the mayor's office, etc. (It's always nice seeing old friends when you're out of work.)

Or you might try widening your strike until every professional prosti-tute is on strike from coast to coast.

I don't know how else you can cause a congressional investigation.

Dear Mark Edwards:

Do we have any legal standing at this point in preventing the public schools from teaching our son their version of sex education?

Sex Preventative

Dear Prophylactic:

Maybe you can teach your son okay, but how do you know who is teaching what to the girl down the street?

Dear Mark Edwards:

I'm nearing 80, but who says old ladies don't have as much sexual interest in men as we ever had?

And I don't mean old men.

I have as much sexual interest in old men as I ever had—not much! It's terrible that young men don't pay attention to old ladies.

No Foolin'

Dear No Foolin':

Why don't you give some of the older fellas a chance?

I've always heard, the older the bird, the more seasoning you need.

June 1

TO: Mark Edwards
FROM: Owen Hatch
News/Features Syndicate

Perhaps you're right.

Carry on.

But try to be a little more selective.

Sorry to foist our Ms. Halamay on you, Mark, but we had to get her out of Chicago to evade charges of Exhibitionism and Public Lewdness.

I should have told you. Never take her bowling.

Something about candlepins makes her take off all her clothes and dance erotically, leaping from alley to alley.

First time she did it, we were able to cover it up (you might say).

Second time, we reassigned her to you.

Any bowling alleys near your office?

11.

June 11

Dear ME:

Women!

Children!

Cops and robbers!

Nothing is what it's *supposed to be*!

Apparently our Ms. Halamay, the Illinois Exhibitionist, does not get it off by answering the phone, and therefore she never does.

Of course it rings all the time—people who just want to say they agree with me; people who just want to say they disagree with me; people who think I'm funny; people who think they're funny; people who want me to plug their latest inspirational book (they all seem to be entitled UP AND AT 'EM!); people who can't find pen and paper to write me; people who have never owned pen and paper; people who really wanted to talk to Buzz

Hodd, in the sports department, and got the wrong number; other drunks, creeps, kooks, and sickies—all, obviously, with whom our publicly lewd Ms. Halamay should speak.

But, no, our Ms. Halamay is as evasive of a ringing telephone as she is of a summons to appear in an Illinois Criminal District Court.

Once—once!—in annoyance, glaring through the glass wall at Ms. Halamay's skinny backside as she opened mail in the outer office, I answered the phone.

"Is this Mr. Mark Edwards?"

"Who is calling, please?"

"Chief Bracknell, Serene, North Carolina."

"Siren?"

"Serene. Like calm."

"On Lake Calm?"

"Is Mr. Edwards there?"

"Mr. Bricknell—"

"Chief Bracknell—"

"What are you chief of?"

"Police."

"I see. Well, Chief, what you're supposed to do is write Mark Edwards a letter, you see, instead of calling him, and his staff goes through the letters and selects, might select yours, and he might, you see, choose your letter to answer in his column. That's how it works. Like dropping a penny in a slot, you never know what might happen. We can't accept phone calls."

"This is personal."

"Well, many say that, Chief, when they call. DEAR MARK EDWARDS is a personal kind of column—"

"We have his son in custody."

After a long pause I heard myself say, "What?"

"We have Mark Edwards, Junior, in custody. May I please speak with Mr. Edwards?"

"Wait a minute, Chief."

In role, I should have said, "One moment, please, I'll see if Mr. Edwards is in," or something, but what I meant, and what I said, was, "Wait a minute, Chief."

I put the receiver down on the desk blotter, weak-armed, and took a deep breath.

Military Markey, the Curious Cadet.

In custody?

"Hello," I said into the phone. "Is my son all right?"

"He's all right, Mr. Edwards." The Chief's voice hadn't changed. For him, this was a routine phone call. I guess I hadn't changed my voice, either. He must have known he was talking to the same person. The same phony. "He has a cut on the forearm, but we've taken care of that."

"Did you say he's in custody?"

"Yes, sir."

Rage gathered up her skirts from the four corners of the world and entered my gut.

Mark arrested? My son arrested?

Who would arrest him? Why?

Rage bellowed through my nose: "On what charge?"

"Breaking and entering."

"B and E?"

I might as well let him know immediately I had spent some of my life covering the police beat.

"Yes, sir."

Goddamned cops.

"I want to speak to the arresting officer, please."

"He's off duty at the moment, Mr. Edwards."

"And when will he be on duty?"

"Not until midnight tonight."

"I want to know what evidence you have that my son broke into and entered any place."

Rage and her little pal, Fear, had succeeded in changing my voice.

"Because your son is thirteen years old, Mr. Edwards, there will be a hearing in Judge Tuckerman's chambers at ten-thirty tomorrow morning. We delayed the hearing twenty-four hours to give the boy a chance to catch up with himself and, of course, to give us time to contact you."

I paused.

I said, "Yes."

"In case you'd like to have a lawyer present."

"Lawyer! I'll be there myself. I'll be there quicker than you can pop the top of a can of soda."

"Sir?"

"Where the hell is . . ."

"Serene, North Carolina."

"Serene, North Carolina?"

"Lots of people ask that."

"I'm sure lots of people have reason to."

"We're the town next to Mount Ada. West of it. Sort of a resort town. Your son attends the Mount Ada Military Academy?"

"I know that."

"We don't have an airport of our own, but Mount Ada has a little one."

"I know that, too. And listen here, Chief What's-Your-Name—"

"Bracknell."

"Ass is gonna fry. . . ."

Rage was twirling her skirts in my belly.

"Mr. Edwards?"

"What?"

"I understand you're upset. We'll see you in the morning."

"You'll see me before then."

I hung up.

I was surprised to discover that sometime during the conversation I had stood up.

The phone receiver sat smugly in its cradle, as if it were absolutely innocent of treachery, in and of itself.

Son of a bitch.

"Ms. Halamay!"

She toothpicked her way into my office.

No wonder she was charged with Exhibitionism and Public Lewdness.

Did she expect anyone to cheer if she took off her clothes?

"Get me to Serene, North Carolina, as quickly as possible."

"This came for you by special messenger."

She handed me a blank envelope.

My name wasn't even on it.

I hadn't seen anyone enter the office.

"I said Serene, North Carolina. It's near Mount Ada."

"You mean, by phone?"

"By plane. Wagon train. Mule. Get me there as quick as you can. Also, what paper in that area runs my column?"

Inside the envelope was a single ticket to a baseball game. Odd there was only one. Ducats usually come in pairs. A box seat. July twenty-third. My birthday. I'd be on the Island then. I stuck it in my wallet anyway.

Dear ME: you see what happens? The one phone call I answer tells me Markey has been arrested; instead of that one call being some crank with some foolishness, or something as irrelevant to the rage, to the fear, to the logistical problems of the moment as a ticket to a baseball game coincidentally on my birthday sneaking into my office by special messenger.

Life isn't serious. It can't be!

Ms. Halamay had written down "Serene—Mount Ada, No. Carolina" on her pad.

"Quick," I said. "Find out what newspaper—"

She went back to her own desk.

Wouldn't any decent, sensible co-worker, assistant, express some interest, some curiosity, some concern as to why I, Mark Edwards, *dear Mark Edwards,* suddenly had to dash to Serene, North Carolina?

Accident in the family?

Yes, goddamn it!

Son of a bitch!

Which reminded me to call Markey's mother. Dear Merriam Edwards.

We had another civil conversation.

I said, "Markey's been arrested and charged with breaking and entering in Serene, North Carolina."

After a five-beat silence, she said, "Your phrasing is impeccable."

"I'm leaving for North Carolina right now."

I hung up.

Merriam could roll with the punch.

Originally, Mark Edwards, Junior, had been in her custody.

Bitch.

Ms. Halamay entered, reading from her pad.

"You can make connections to Winston-Salem, but from there you need to charter a plane."

"Do so. What newspaper—"

"The Mount Ada *Dispatch.*"

"Please call the managing editor of the Mount Ada *Dispatch* and ask him to have someone meet my plane. Someone who has contacts in the Serene, North Carolina, police department."

I didn't arrive in Serene until eight-fifteen the next morning. Flights were neither hourly nor direct to Winston-Salem and when I arrived there the pilot of the chartered plane refused to take off until the wind and rain had abated (I could hardly blame him [but I did]; landing had been like being let down in that notorious cradle from that notorious tree when the wind blew), so that meant hanging around in a corner of that airport for hours.

So I arrived in Serene damp, unkempt, tired, and with nerves ajangle from too much coffee.

Fuck serenity.

And the *Dispatch* had sent a copy boy/cub reporter to pick me up in a small, rotted-out Ford.

Nevertheless, I asked him, "Who do you know in the Serene police department?"

He knew how to start the car.

"Chief Bracknell. Sort of."

"What have you got on him?"

He did not know how to shift into first gear.

"You mean, against him?"

"Yeah."

Or from first into second.

"He's sort of a nice guy."

"You're a big help."

Or from second into third.

"You know where the police station is?"

"I can find it."

He also didn't know how to brake.

"You're Mark Edwards?" he asked.

"Yeah." He commenced shifting practice again. I said, "You'd like a column like mine someday?"

Thought I might try to make a friend somewhere.

"No, sir," he answered somewhat uncomfortably, I thought. "I'd rather get more into journalism. . . ."

"Let's see if we can get to the police station."

Which was in the basement of the Town Building.

The desk cop said, "I expect you'd like to see your son first? Before you see the Chief?"

"Of course."

Actually, it had been my first idea to break the head of every cop in Serene, North Carolina.

The cell was clean, didn't smell, and was big enough to make Markey look awfully young and small.

He sat on the edge of his bunk in the posture of dejection humans learn to adopt almost immediately after birth. Or so it seems.

He was in the dark blue academy uniform, without the tie. His shoes were dusty and looked too big for him. Too big for anybody.

There was a hank of hair down Markey's forehead and pimples on his chin.

I said, "You jerk. Haven't you learned anything at that Military School?"

"Yeah," he said. "Not to get caught."

His right sleeve was rolled up. There were bandages on his forearm.

"I guess I'm just not a quick study," he said. "Slow learner. Very slow."

"Did you have anything to do with this . . . this crime?"

"Sure."

"You did?"

"Yeah."

"Why?"

"I wanted a camera," he said. "I wanted a hi-fi. I also wanted the money."

"Jesus."

"You shouldn't swear in front of kids."

"I'm praying! What am I supposed to do?"

"I dunno," he said. "Take it like a man, I guess."

"Let me outa here."

Chief Bracknell seemed decent enough. He'd shaved.

He offered me coffee.

Sitting in his office, I said, "I'd like to talk to the arresting officer."

"I thought you'd say that."

"Before the hearing."

"I also thought you'd say that."

"I'd like to know the facts."

"Of course."

"I'd also like to explain to him—"

"Of course." The Chief made himself comfortable in his chair. "In this case, I'm going to say no."

"No?"

He lit a cigarette and said, "I shouldn't smoke."

I didn't care if he burned.

"In this case, Mr. Edwards, I think we have more to explain to you than you have to explain to us. I've talked with the boy a bit. I'm a father myself. You and the boy's mother are divorced?"

"Everybody's divorced."

"I'm not."

"Yeah, but you smoke."

"I smoke and I drink and sometimes on Saturdays I beat people over the head with a nightstick. But I'm not divorced."

"You want to jail my son because his father's divorced?"

"Your son needs help."

"I'll give him help."

"You haven't."

"His mother got custody."

"His father's got a son."

"Chief, you trying to tell me I've ignored my son? I'm a negligent father?"

He fiddled with the cigarette pack on his desk blotter. "Somethin' like that."

"Chief, in a couple of weeks, next month, when the kids get out of school, we're all going on a family vacation, I've got a big summer place out on the Island—"

"Mr. Edwards, I don't know precisely what your life is like, I'm just a tarheel, an old boy who drinks sody from the can. . . . I know you're a columnist. I read your column, sometimes you can be right kindly. You remarried?"

"Yes."

"Your boy tells me that you and your current wife have four children between you, and the apartment you live in only has two bedrooms."

"The kids are never home."

He lit another cigarette.

"If you didn't want kids, why in hell did you have 'em?"

"My wife works. I work."

"My wife answers the phone over at the high school."

"My wife is Pamela Jensen."

"Oh, yeah. You might tell her I agree with that review she wrote in *Hawthorne's* last week, on the movie *1984*?"

"Christ. I'd like to see your evidence."

" 'Bout the same as hers—"

"I'm talking about the breaking-and-entering charge."

"Oh. Yeah. Well, your boy was caught red-handed in Stabler's Hi-Fi and Camera Equipment store at twenty minutes to twelve night before last by Officer Morton."

"What was Officer Morton doing there?"

"Responding to a silent alarm."

"Oh. Is there any evidence, other than Officer Morton's word, that Mark was actually in the store?"

"Yes, sir. The window that was smashed had blood on it. Your son had a cut forearm. The blood types matched."

"Oh. What evidence is there Mark had the intent to commit robbery?"

"Officer Morton found him with a smashed cashbox in his hands and one hundred and twenty-one dollars in his pockets. You give him that much allowance?"

"Oh."

"You say 'Oh' a lot. Guess I can't blame you."

"Chief, this is Mark's first offense."

"Actually, it's not. But I thought you'd think so."

"What do you mean?"

"Your boy has been in to the station a couple of times before."

"On what charges?"

"Shoplifting."

"Shit. Shit shit shit."

"And you never knew it."

The school never told me. Merriam never told me!

"As I say, Mr. Edwards, I don't know your way of life, precisely, but I suspect it has to do with late dinner parties and slow mornings. I suspect you play with power the way us folks down here play with time. All depends on what you enjoy in this life. I appreciate your not trying to play with power down here." He twitched the venetian blind behind his head. "I saw that you drove up in one of the cars of the Mount Ada *Dispatch*. . . ."

Power taken from me, understood away from me, I suffered time in my chair.

Time was awful.

The Chief looked at his watch. "I expect they'll be taking your boy up to Judge Tuckerman's chambers about now." He stood up. "I'll go through this with you."

In time, I stood up.

"Thing is," the Chief said, "your boy is in our hands now, legally. Whether he put himself purposely there or not, I don't know."

"You're a psychiatrist?"

"No, sir. But neither are you."

We all sat in Judge Tuckerman's chambers. Markey. Myself. Arresting Officer Morton (who looked decent enough; he'd shaved). Judge Tuckerman behind his desk. Silently, Chief Bracknell sat to one side, smoking.

Everyone was horribly nice.

Chummy.

Officer Morton went through the evidence.

It would have been an easy story to write.

I hoped the Mount Ada *Dispatch* wouldn't pick up the story.

Judge Tuckerman asked Mark what he had to say.

Mark said nothing, and looked at me.

I tried.

I said how great Mount Ada Military Academy had been for Mark.

(Bastards hadn't even told me about the shoplifting charges.)

I said how much his mother, Merriam, loves him.

(Neither had that bitch told me.)

I said how much his stepmother, Pamela, loves him.

(I had never realized we only had a two-bedroom apartment before. And four children!)

I described the family vacation we had all planned, the big old house out on the Island.

It all sounded pretty hollow, even to me.

As hollow as a summer house in winter.

Chummy. Chummy.

Mark will be allowed to finish the school year at Mount Ada. He will spend the summer at a North Carolina youth psychiatric diagnostic center with the hope a therapy course will be begun which will allow him to attend school next fall. He will remain on court probation until Judge Tuckerman is satisfied his problems have been psychiatrically resolved.

How goddamned modern this world has become!

I have spent too long, writing this.

Unable to advise my son, I must get back to advising the World.

June 14

Dear Mark Edwards:

Our Committee would appreciate your expressing your views in your column concerning violence on television.

Our view is that constant violence on television encourages increasing violence in our lives and is largely responsible for the worldwide annual increase in crime rates.

Lillian Odell, Pres.
Television-Terrible
Committee

P.S. We trust, now that your column is syndicated, your answer will be more responsible.

June 15

Dear Mark Edwards:

The oddest thing is beginning to happen to me—well, is happening to me.

You know how it is when you miss, very much, someone you love and he's in your mind alot, and every time you're in some sort of a crowd, or the street or something, you keep thinking you're seeing him, suddenly alot of people walk and talk and dress and look just like him? And even though your friend is out of the country, or something, it's impossible for him to be right there just then, you run after the stranger in the street or in the store, ready to say hello and hug and kiss until you get up real close and discover he's not who you thought he is at all?

Well, the same thing is happening to me.

Except the person I keep seeing is me!

First time, I was on a bus, rainy day, and I saw me walking along the sidewalk. I had the impulse to get off the bus and run after me.

A few days later, when I was leaving a building, I turned around in the lobby and saw me waiting for an elevator.

I was buying perfume, and I looked across and there was someone I wanted to greet as me at another counter buying gloves!

I thought I should write you because this morning, when I was waiting to cross the street, three of the people waiting to cross over to my side looked like me. I'm getting used to it. I looked away. And standing right next to me was a person who was my spitting image!

Do I just accept this situation?

>Everybody
>(Grace Keddy)

June 19

Dear Ms. Keddy:

This sensation you report having with increasing frequency is psychiatrically symptomatic, and I suggest you talk it over with one or two psychiatrists, and see what they say.

Don't worry about doing so—almost everyone can benefit from therapy.

And—how do you know?—you might find a psychiatrist who looks just like you!

>Love Never Faileth,
>Mark Edwards

June 19

Dear Mark Edwards:

I would like to know the personal effect upon you of writing the DEAR MARK EDWARDS column.

>Sincerely,
>Dr. Frank Miller

June 17

Dear Mark Edwards:

Your column—and everything else one reads these days—seems to be about, and for, beautiful, sexy people.

And the only thing you people ever seem to say is Relax and Enjoy! Go to bed together!

What about all us people who are really ugly, and can't help it? How are we supposed to Relax, and Enjoy?

From the Deep
(Stella Putnam)

June 22

Dear Ms. Putnam:

I find that humans are mostly a little better—a little brighter, a little richer, a little more attractive—than we think we are. (Except for me, of course!)

It has to be so.

Our image of ourselves is formed mostly by how other people react to us, and what they have to say about us.

The simplest way of their putting themselves up in their own eyes (they suffer, too) is by putting us down.

Growing up, walking around, being alive, we get insulted much, much more than we get complimented.

Ergo, we have to be better than we think we are.

Right?

Relax and Enjoy.

Love Never Faileth,
Mark Edwards

(June 23)

Dear Mark Edwards:

Everywhere I look—in the bus, on the street, in stores, office buildings—everyone looks like me!

Am I losing my mind?

Everybody

Dear Everybody:

Having trouble telling yourself apart, eh?

Gee, and I thought everybody looks like me!

Do you suppose you and I look alike?

Dear Mark Edwards:

Our Committee would appreciate your expressing your views in your column concerning violence on television.

Television-Terrible
Committee

Dear Television-Terrible Committee:

Being confronted, hour after hour, day after day, week after week, month after month, year after year, with endlessly repetitious incidents of assault, rape, murder, and other violent crime on our most passive medium, television, has to have the most damaging effect upon us, particularly the young.

Having such depictions of violent, criminal behavior consume such a large part of our attention has to cause us to consider such behavior more normal, more acceptable than it is—more the rule than the exception.

Although humans are basically violent, I believe the effect of constant violence on television is to lower the threshold, the barrier, between socially acceptable and unacceptable behavior.

Certainly our courts are full of good kids who have done bad deeds, without their fully realizing what they were doing.

Something must be twisting their heads.

Dear Mark Edwards:

Everything you read these days seems to be about, and for, beautiful, sexy people.

What about all us plug-uglies?

From the Deep

Dear From the Deep:

Show me someone who isn't plug-ugly and I'll show you someone who's hired a public relations firm.

Dear Mark Edwards:

Our teen-aged son has been convicted of a serious crime and we cannot come to grips with it. He has always been such a good boy.

Are we to blame? Can a boy change so much, from good to bad, so suddenly? Will we ever be able to relate to him, really relate to him again, as the son we once knew and loved?

Aghast

Dear Aghast:

Forgive him.

Forgive yourselves.

Find ways of going forward.

12.

Dear Mark Edwards:
   I have this problem: I think my penis is too short.
   What shall I do, pull it?

                                   Short Fuse
                                   (Chas. Ruthazer)

                                        July 3

Dear Mr. Ruthazer:
   You'd have better luck, I think, if you got someone else to pull it.

                                   Love Never Faileth,
                                   Mark Edwards

                                        June 28

Dear Mr. Edwards:
   You are not my friend, and distinctly not, I repeat, not my Daddy. I don't even know you well enough to know if you dodder.

I have only the slightest impression of you, from my having been present at your wedding to my mother, and that impression was not favorable. You seemed to have the belief you had every right to be there, doing what you were doing.

My main impression of you is from your column—which is a disgrace and an embarrassment. No one here at Princeton knows you have the temporary right to call yourself my stepfather. The possibility of anyone's finding out gives me nightmares.

However, my humor is such that I have not been able to resist writing a satire of your column for the fall issue of the college humor magazine. I'll send you a copy, if you haven't changed your address by then.

My first year at Princeton has taught me I ought to answer letters that seem to require answering.

You may take your volleyball, your tennis racket, your sailboat, your house on the island, and stick them up your nose, while singing Parting Songs from as much of the operatic repertoire as is at your command.

The simplest inquiry would have informed you I'm spending the summer—all of it—here at a ranch in British Columbia.

Sincerely,
Jason Jensen

July 3

Dear Jason:

There's nothing more sophomoric than a satire of a satire.

Love Never Faileth,
Mark Edwards

June 27

Dear Mark Edwards:

Maybe your publishing this letter will carry on my ministry.

I have been minister for eleven years in a small suburban town, where the congregation has above-average wealth and education.

For eleven years I built and maintained my family in this community, on little money and with even less privacy, while counseling these people, as a congregation, as family groups, peer groups, individually, heart to heart and soul to soul. Seldom have they failed to bring to me their indiscretions, sins, cruelties, stupidities, anxieties, hurts, and never have I turned them away or failed to try to understand them.

Maybe I have taken on their sins, or, been seduced by them.

Less and less, in this wealthy, materialistic society, my wife saw herself as a minister's wife. I guess she became bored with me.

At the same time, there was a woman in the congregation who had lost her husband tragically. First, I counseled her. She was of such spiritual beauty that soon I began drawing on her strength. We became friends. She counseled me. And, yes, we became intimate.

My wife came to know about this and, as she was looking for an excuse to divorce me anyway, I guess, did so.

The divorce; the "other woman": six months ago the congregation fired me. (But not until after I gave them a sermon, saying, "Let him among you who is without sin throw the first stone." I got clobbered—pelted with stones.)

No wife, no family, no church, no job.

What hurts so much is that, despite my best efforts, I failed to teach my congregation understanding and forgiveness.

Johnny Gaiters
(Rev. Robert Henley)

July 3

Dear Dr. Henley:

There are still a great many "double standards" in this world. A double standard is intrinsic to the ministry.

If you allow a community to set you up as some kind of an ideal, a model, and it is this prestige which allows you to live and do your work among them, you must realize that if you lose it, you lose everything.

You allowed the community to tell itself a lie about you, and, when the lie was discovered, you all lost.

You might consider beginning a ministry based on no lies whatsoever.

That would be refreshing.

Love Never Faileth,
Mark Edwards

June 26

Dear Mark Edwards:

The only good thing about clothes is pockets.

If it weren't for pockets (and the Law) I wouldn't wear any clothes. Who needs 'em?

Have you noticed how pockets seem to be disappearing from clothes?

At least the clothes my wife keeps buying me.

First, the wristwatch did away with the watch pocket. Then the change pockets disappeared from both trousers and jackets. Then one of the inside jacket pockets disappeared. Try to buy a vest with pockets you can use. Next, one, then both shirt pockets disappeared. Trousers got more "form-fitting" or something, but goddamnit, the front pockets got five inches shorter, and one of the back pockets disappeared! My new suit has no back pockets in the trousers, front pockets that are so shallow I can't keep change in them without dripping quarters and dimes when I sit down, and no outside pockets in the jacket whatsoever!

I find myself walking down the street with a pack of cigarettes in one hand and my wallet in the other.

So what does my wife do?

She buys me a handbag! With a shoulder strap!

Who stole my pockets?

I want my pockets back!

> Pocketless
> (Harry LaBreque)

July 3

Dear Mr. LaBreque:

Enclosed: one (1) pocket.

> Love Never Faileth,
> Mark Edwards

June 30

Dear "Dad":

Thanks for your invite to your birthday party, but as Mum has probably told you, I have a chance to work on the piano with Lydia Kaufmann this summer, at her place in Woodstock. You know I won that competition? It's a rare opportunity.

Guess you'll have to turn forty without me. Thanks anyway.

Love,
Pam (Jensen)

July 3

Dear Pam:

Right.

Congratulations on winning the competition. Your mother and I are both very proud of you.

Have a great summer with Madame Kaufmann.

Be sure and take some time for yourself, just to have fun.

Love Never Faileth,
"Dad"

July 5

Dear ME:

Pamela Jensen invited me out to dinner.

What's more, I went.

We each ordered a vodka gimlet.

On that, we agreed.

I had spent the afternoon televising a commercial, doing each take forty times. I was being paid munificently to endorse the United States Postal Service. ("The answer's in the mail!" I had declaimed cheerily one hundred and sixty odd times that afternoon.) The fee would keep me in stamps for life.

I was tired.

My shirt was still damp from sweat.

Even though I had washed, the stuff they had put on my face to help me look cheery was still sticky and smelly.

Finally out with Pamela (although I had arrived late), a quiet, pleasant, noncontroversial dinner would have been acceptable to me. Would have made all the difference.

Would have been impossible.

She said, "I see you've been getting more mail from your ex-wife."

And instead of saying, What?, I shivered and said, "Who?"

(If people thoroughly grasped, understood all the mistakes I actually make under their very noses, my life wouldn't be worth living at all.)

"Merriam."

"Oh."

"Only this time you signed her 'Aghast.' "

"I thought it would be a help to her."

"Mark, you do not have the right to use your column as a means of beating up those near and dear to you."

"Who's beating up? I wrote that letter to help her. It's what I would have said to her if I'd been able. In person. Forgive Markey. Forgive yourself. Go forward."

"Mark, you don't have the right to write letters for anybody. Or from anybody. Or to anybody, for that matter. Who says Merriam needs you to tell her to forgive her son? Or herself?"

"Have you heard from her again?"

"No."

"Then who, Pamela Jensen, are you to speak for her?"

I have noticed that in the very best restaurants the waiters are trained to approach the table and serve only during dramatic pauses. How that instinct is developed in them I can't guess. They must be given a course in face-reading. Wait until Madame is glowering before bringing the drinks.

Madame was glowering and the waiter brought our drinks.

"Say, listen," I said, "I wrote the kids, all of them, yours and mine, ours, about going out to the Island for the two weeks—"

"You did?"

"I did."

"You invited them?"

"Of course."

"You mean you actually took that house?"

"Yes. I said I was going to."

"You said you might."

"I said I did. I asked you to drive out with me and look at it—"

"About six hours before my *Hawthorne's* deadline."

"I can't remember everybody's deadlines."

"I'm not everybody. I'm your wife."

"Anyway, you didn't come."

"I thought you didn't want me to go with you. Why else would you ask me at such an inconvenient time?"

"Pamela, I don't know what is a convenient time."

"And you took the house? You actually rented the house?"

"Yes."

"When you came back, you didn't say anything."

"I didn't say anything because I took the house. I thought it was understood."

"Well, it wasn't. And it isn't."

"I wrote the kids—"

"What dates?"

"What dates did I write the kids? I don't remember. In plenty of time."

"I mean, for what dates did you rent the house?"

"Oh. From the fifteenth on."

"This month? July?"

"Yes."

"From the fifteenth of July to the first of August?"

"Yes."

"Mark, you know I have to be on the Coast those two weeks."

"No. I didn't know."

"I'm on the Coast every year the last two weeks of July."

"I guess I forgot."

"Like hell you did. That's when they show us the new product, the films for fall and winter release."

"Okay, I forgot."

"You also know I was going to stay out there and work on my book. The manuscript is due right after Labor Day."

"No. I did not know that."

"What the hell is the significance of the last two weeks of July?"

My legs were tired from doing the commercial. My shirt was damp and uncomfortable. My face was beginning to itch from the makeup, which must be advertised to adhere twenty-four hours whether you want it to or not.

"I'll tell you what the significance of the last two weeks of July is," Pamela said. "If I don't get out to California and learn the new releases at that point, I'm about cooked for the year.

You resent my job, and you always have. Now you have enough of an income to support yourself, this is your way of sabotaging me."

"Oh, my God."

"Why don't you stop scratching your face?"

"You're tormenting me."

"There's no way I'm going to the Island the last two weeks of July. No way."

"I've got the point."

"What did the kids say?"

"Oh." I realized I hadn't touched my drink. "Jason's out in British Columbia already. On a ranch."

"I told you that."

"I don't think you did."

"Next time I'll write you a letter."

" 'Thank you for your letter to the Mark Edwards column. Time does not permit a personal answer. Sincerely, Mark Edwards.' "

"And Pammy's in Woodstock with Mrs. Kaufmann."

"You knew that, too. Did you know she won a competition?"

"I don't make a habit of publishing family news in my column in *Hawthorne's*."

I touched my drink. I drank half of it.

"What's with these kids?" I asked. "They seem so busy."

"Pamela's doing very well with the piano. Jason may become a specialist in the history of the American Indian."

"No one has two weeks in the summer?"

"I'm not going to the Island, Mark. So why should Pammy and Jason?"

"Right."

"They barely know you."

"Right."

"And neither one of them has had to spend any time in Reform School."

The woman who made that comment was sitting across the table from me.

She was my wife.

"In jail," she said.

My wife, Pamela Jensen.

I swallowed the rest of my drink and sat back in my chair.

Pamela Jensen. So used to being the slashing critic. Jumping up and down in ten-league boots, victoriously, on the little gardens of other people's dreams, ideas, works, lives. For her, the slashing line was an achievement.

"I'm sorry," she said. "I feel bad about Markey, too. Do you want another drink?"

The vibrations from our table had been so bad the well-trained waiter had brought us menus.

I put mine aside.

"That, Pamela Jensen," I said, "just about does it."

"I know," she said. "That was a low blow."

"Many things have been crystallizing for me lately. Are crystallizing. Maybe it's the column that's doing it for me, partly. Reading all these crazy letters, thinking about the people who write them, trying to answer them. At first, I thought the letters would drive me bananas. But after four months of it, I find I'm beginning to think quite naturally in terms of pain, confusion, anxiety, fear, genuine, individual injustice, selfishness, cruelty."

"I want another drink, if you don't."

"Have it."

The waiter had not gone far from us.

"But it's not only the column," I said. "This cop in North Carolina, Chief Bracknell, is really a very nice guy. He was very good and kind and understanding with me—under very difficult circumstances. He hardly knew Markey and me, and why should he care about us? It was a routine matter for him; yet he served ideally the way DEAR MARK EDWARDS should: good, kind, understanding, trying to put his thumb on the problem the way sometimes you can from a great distance."

"Listen, Mark, if you want to give a course on How to Write a Lovelice Column, maybe City University—"

"Chief Bracknell pointed out something interesting to me, something I had never realized before. You know what it was?"

Pamela was exchanging glasses with the waiter, treating him to her modest-celebrity grin.

"Chief Bracknell, this cop in North Carolina, pointed out we live in a two-bedroom apartment and have four kids."

Pamela finished her shtick with her drink slowly before looking at me and saying, "Yes?"

I said nothing.

She said, "We have one bedroom for ourselves, and one bedroom for the children."

"They never come."

"They're busy, Mark."

"We have just enough space for them in our apartment to assuage our conscience—your conscience—but not enough space for any one, or any combination of them, to think that they are welcome, that that is their space."

"Well, you see, Mark, we've had this financial problem," she said, brightly. "Four very expensive children, and not all that much income, between the two of us—"

I stood up.

"Pamela: why have we had only two bedrooms for ourselves and four children?"

"Where are you going, Mark?"

I leaned over and kissed her.

"Good night, Pamela. I'm going to a hotel."

(July 7)

Dear Mark Edwards:

The only good thing about clothes is pockets.

If it weren't for pockets (and the Law) I wouldn't wear any clothes. Who needs 'em?

Have you noticed how pockets seem to be disappearing from clothes?

First the watch pocket, then the change pockets, then an inside-jacket pocket, first one shirt pocket, then the other, a pants back pocket, the front pants pockets got five inches shorter, then both pants back pockets!

To hell with men's fashions!

I want my pockets back!

Pocketless

Dear Pocketless:

What I do (as all of us who wish to be well turned out are confronted with this problem of pocketlessness) is tie ropes tightly around my trousers legs and jacket sleeves at the ankles and wrists.

And then I fill up the pant legs and sleeves with whatever I want to carry.

Granted, I clank and crinkle somewhat as I walk, and my best friends tell me I look bunchy.

But no one can say I'm not dressed in the height of current fashion!

Dear Mark Edwards:

I had my summer plans all made out and now I discover my parents expect me to go on a vacation with them!

How do I tell them?

Pum-Pum

Dear Pum-Pum:

Simply and directly is the kindest way to tell anybody anything.

Even so, they'll miss you.

Are you sure your summer plans are so important you can't spend a couple of weeks with the old folks?

Dear Mark Edwards:

For 11 years, as minister in this suburban community, members of my congregation have been bringing me their indiscretions, sins, cruelties, stupidities, anxieties, hurts. Never have I turned them away or failed to try to understand them.

There was a woman in the congregation who lost her husband tragically. First, I counseled her. She was of such spiritual beauty that soon I began to draw on her strength. We became friends. She counseled me. And, yes, we became intimate.

My wife divorced me.

My congregation fired me.

How, in the 11 years of my ministry, did I fail so utterly in teaching my congregation human understanding, and human forgiveness . . . ?

Johnny Gaiters

Dear Johnny Gaiters:

One doesn't have to be Samuel Johnson to discover Philosophers may think like angels, but must live as men.

13.

Dear Daddy Dodderer:

Thanks for your permission to transfer to St. Axelrood's in the fall. I know some neat kids there already.

Sorry I won't be able to contribute my charm, wit, and other talents to the family bash out on the Island (what Island?) later this month, but Nicky and I mean to trek the Appalachian Trail from the Canadian border south as far as our pins will carry us. I felt I didn't need your permission for this. (After all, Doddering One, you have to admit you owe Nicky *something*. By the way, slugger, his jaw was not permanently impaired, you'll be glad to know, I'm sure. The only words he has difficulty saying are *Mark* and *Edwards*—they come out sort of slurred.)

Besides, it sounds like you're going to have sort of a full house, what with Jason II, Pammy II, Markey II, and Wifey II.

Sorry about my marks this year, but it wasn't a total loss.

After being mystified by Algebra for a whole year, at least I ended up knowing X + N = D.

Shelley

July 14

Dear Shelley:
Thanks for writing the old man on his birthday.
Have fun with Nicky.

Your Doddering Dad

July 23

Dear ME:
The remarkable thing about Life is that, even at forty (maybe, especially at forty) there are surprises, there are still surprises, there are still always surprises.

I didn't know where else to be, and I had to be Mark Edwards celebrating his fortieth birthday somewhere, so I came out here to the house on the Island, alone, last night. The bed sheets were damp, of course, the larder empty, except for a half-bottle of gin and some instant coffee; the house as hollow as lies told in aid of a son in trouble. But there was a new moon over the ocean, a decent breeze on the deck, and enough ice to make the gin potable.

I spent last week, the first week of my vacation, in North Carolina, seeing as much of Markey as the Authorities would allow, which wasn't much (actually, I saw four filums [Pamela had been right about all of them] and read eight books in five days), until their psychologist or whatever had a conference with me (it sure wasn't a conversation) and told me my spending time with Markey at this point, giving him this "unusual attention," was rewarding him for having committed a crime (an "antisocial act," she said) and would only serve to reinforce his subconscious motivation to commit more crimes (more "antisocial acts") subsequently, when he felt, subconsciously, he wasn't receiving adequate attention from me.

The message: Please go away.
So I went.

This morning, about my fourteen thousand, six hundred and fiftieth (think how tickled François Marie Arouet de Voltaire would have been to have had the time and solitude to figure out such a triviality), I rose with the sun (there were no shades in the bedroom), took my imitation coffee out onto the sundeck, found the ocean more or less where I'd left it, studied the swirls on the sand (they were pretty good, in design, but a little careless in execution), watched a lonely figure (a man about my age) walking along the edge of the water far up the beach, remembered I had last eaten in the airport in Winston-Salem, many states away, and drove myself into the village for a breakfast of scrambled eggs, sausages, and home fries.

"Forevermore is shorter than before."

Gee.

Gee.

I did not buy a newspaper. I had not read any newspaper, even the Mount Ada *Dispatch*, since my vacation had begun. I did not want to see what Ms. Halamay was doing with DEAR MARK EDWARDS. Doubtless everyone was being advised to consult with their local shrinks, ministers, rabbis, priests, and to keep his or her pants on. (She should know.)

Therefore it was a great surprise when I returned to the house to discover a car from the newspaper office had snuck in and out like an Easter rabbit leaving me, on my doorstep, instead of a May basket, two sacksful of telegrams.

I knelt on the porch and read some of them, starting with the one pinned conspicuously to the outside of one of the sacks.

MARK EDWARDS:

BIRTHDAY GREETINGS FROM BOTH MY WIFE AND MYSELF ON YOUR FORTIETH. MAY YOU CONTINUE CREATING HUMAN UNDERSTANDING THROUGH YOUR COLUMN "DEAR MARK EDWARDS."

THE WHITE HOUSE
WASHINGTON, D.C.

(As a taxpayer, I would have appreciated it more if he had stayed within the word limit.)

MARK EDWARDS:

BIRTHDAY GREETINGS FROM BOTH MY WIFE AND MYSELF ON YOUR FORTIETH. BEST WISHES FOR THE CONTINUED SUCCESS OF DEAR MARK EDWARDS.

> MONROE LIPTON,
> PUBLISHER

(All he's making off me, he can afford to go over the limit.)

MARK EDWARDS:

ESCAPED. TO PROVE TO YOU PERSONALLY I ONLY SLASH FACES. ON YOUR FORTIETH.

> JUMBO DONDERSHINE

MARK EDWARDS:

HAPPY BIRTHDAY. WISH TO KNOW PERSONAL EFFECT UPON YOU OF YOUR COLUMN.

> DR. FRANK MILLER

MARK EDWARDS:

HOPE YOU LEARN MORE YOUR NEXT FORTY THAN YOU DID YOUR LAST.

> DONALD BAINBRIDGE

MARK EDWARDS:

BEING FORTY BEATS ALL HECK OUT OF THE ALTERNATIVE. I THINK.

> BILL COSBY

"What is this?" I expostulated into Owen Hatch's ear through the phone.

"What's what?"

I had had to wait for Chicago to wake up, then for News/Features Syndicate to wake up, then for Owen Hatch to wake up and get to his desk.

"All these telegrams—"

"Oh, yeah. Happy birthday."

"These telegrams—"

"I asked Jim Krikorian to send 'em out to you. How many did you get?"

"Hundreds."

"Oh, well. You'll probably get more."

He wasn't satisfied with "hundreds."

"Haven't you been reading your column?" he asked.

(Lamely:) "I've been away."

"We've been shirttailing it all week with the news today is your birthday."

"Why?"

"Today is your fortieth birthday, isn't it?"

"Shit, Owen, a birthday's a private matter. A family matter."

"Hell, Mark, it's good public relations for you to have a birthday."

"Whaddaya mean?"

"Everybody has birthdays. Men, women, and children. Bankers. Housewives. Neurosurgeons. People in jail, on Skid Row—"

"That's how they got there."

"Birthdays they understand. Pamela Jensen they don't. With birthdays they can identify."

"Why publish it?"

"Involve the reader. Isn't that what you're always saying, Mark? Get the reader involved. Be personal. Once they send you a telegram wishing you happy birthday, they'll read you forever."

"Jesus, Owen."

Trying to stuff my telephone credit card back into my wallet, I found its slot obstructed by a piece of cardboard.

"Hey, Mark?"

"Yeah?"

I pulled the obstruction out and looked at it.

A ticket to a baseball game.

Box seat.

Today's date.

"Ms. Halamay tells me you're compulsive about answering your mail. I mean, personally."

" 'The answer's in the mail,' " I said.

Where did I get the baseball ticket?

"Don't try to answer all these telegrams."

"I couldn't. I couldn't possibly."

"Good boy. How's the family?"

"Fine."

"Having a nice vacation?"

"Sure."

"Okay, Mark. In case it hasn't been said before: Happy Birthday."

"Thanks a glob."

No matter how I studied it, in the dark, woody living room, in the sunlight on the deck, the baseball ticket would not tell me whence or from whom it came.

How could I have a ticket to a baseball game in my wallet?

Had I put it there?

Somehow I associated it with Chief Bracknell, in North Carolina.

He was a nice guy, but we hadn't talked about baseball.

I associated it with the phone call about Markey.

None of that made sense.

It was a perfectly good ticket, and there was no kid around to give it to. . . .

To the baseball game I went.

I was only dimly aware of them, when they entered the box.

The box had been empty, beautiful seats right on the first base line.

I had been in plenty of time, done my ancient tricks of prediction on the scorecard at the back of the program, stuffed down a hot dog with everything and a beer and then another hot dog with everything and another beer and was pretty well warmed up, tie loose, jacket over the back of my chair, by the top of the second inning, yelling at the lawyer's representative who was pitching, the lawyer's representatives who were batting, the shyster who was umpiring at first. I had already given the lawyer's representative who was managing the home team one piece of my advice, loudly (he would have been better off to have followed my predictions), and had plenty more advice to give him.

The woman was sitting beside me; the man, the other side of her.

I had noticed her suit. Extremely well tailored. Beige.

Pretty brown shoes.

The man and the woman were strangely quiet.

So the clown whose lawyer was being paid to manage my team expressed a general desire for a sacrifice and, boy, did he get one, right between the eyes, a double out.

"Boo!" I said, with great sincerity. Without any wax at all. "Boo! Boo! Boo! Why don't you let your lawyer manage everything, you idiot!"

The side was retiring, but I wasn't.

"Lookit that!" I said to the woman sitting next to me.

Mona Lisa.

Lisa del Gioconda.

That same patient look in the eyes.

That same smile.

The Eternal Face of Woman, Waiting for Man to Catch Up to Her.

Over her shoulder, I saw the man, the young man, also looking at me.

Was I being a disgrace?

On two beers?

Who cares?

I am Mark Edwards.

At a baseball game.

On my birthday.

My fortieth birthday.

I could yell a little.

What else are birthdays and baseball for?

My stomach lurched.

For what were the man and the woman waiting?

For what was she waiting?

I took off my sunglasses and looked at her.

Violet eyes. Her skin was a color and texture I had known only once before. It belonged on an angel, or some other, even more exalted heavenly creature, and even looking at it was breaking through the walls of existence, transcending life as it is, reality, an essentential experience, a clear view of forever. Her hair was still honey.

I said, "Hi."

I sat like Raggedy Andy, staring at the peanut shells on the gray cement at my feet.

I looked at the field. It was green. The diamond was light brown. Beige. The bases and mound were white. There were players out there, but they moved slowly, making little sense.

The single baseball ticket had arrived at the office in a blank envelope by special messenger the day I heard Markey was in trouble. I had stuffed it in my wallet.

I said, "Wow."

Mari laughed.

So did her young man.

It wasn't because of sore teeth Lisa del Gioconda smiled, as some have thought, or because she was barely able to maintain patience with Leonardo, who was spending a total of four years committing her to canvas.

Clearly, it was because she was seeing her husband, her lover, for the first time in twenty-one years, and waiting for him to see her, recognize her.

A husband.

A lover.

After a while, I said, "Listen, I can't sit here." The baseball game was making no sense to me. Shock's distance had intervened. It was like watching it from the Goodyear blimp. "I have a car." I looked at my watch. "Ever have dinner at three o'clock in the afternoon?"

Mari said, "Often."

Her young man followed us to the parking lot. (At some point, the noise from the stadium behind us [who had hit what? who had caught what?], Mari said, "Mark, this is Clark.")

I put him in the back seat.

"You should have enough room," I said.

Through the rearview mirror, I said to him, "Trust the car isn't too grossly big for your taste."

He was only about twenty.

Beautifully dressed.

Of course.

"It's very comfortable," he said.

"It's a Coupe de Ville," I said. "Rented. It has air conditioning." I turned it on and looked at Mari's legs. "Too much for you?"

"No," she said. "It's fine."

On the way into town I asked Mari if she ran a nightclub and she said, "You've never come," and I said, "How do you know?" and she said, "I'd know."

Her young man in the back seat said nothing.

He sat between us at a table for four in the middle of the big, empty, main dining room at Saunders'. I had never known the restaurant was so big, or could be so empty.

Mari ran a nightclub, three of them, was more beautiful than anything or anybody ever seen, and had an extraordinarily beautiful, handsome, twenty-year-old escort named Clark.

Why did she need him?

She ordered a crab meat salad.

Clark disturbed me.

I would like to know what is the personal effect upon you of Mari's twenty-year-old escort?

He was certainly appealing.

He was tall and slim, superbly dressed (by Mari?), superbly groomed, with a unique expression perpetually on his face, of self-confidence, contentment, spirit expended with lots more spirit to give. He looked like someone who had just had a good fuck and knew the next one was only minutes away. (With Mari?) He had a solid gold bracelet on his slim, tanned left wrist (from Mari?). He moved as gracefully as a young lion in territory undisputably his own.

I was not conscious of ever having been so attracted to a young man before.

What had I written the "Senior Officer"?

. . . maybe you're in love with the son you never had. . . .

I have a son.

. . . or you're in love with the young man you once were. . . .

That was possible.

On a fortieth birthday.

Enjoy love where and how and when you find it.

"I like your column," Mari said. "I guess I wrote you that."

" 'The answer's in the mail,' " I said.

We were all sipping pretty little daiquiris.

"One never knows what advice you're going to write," Mari said. "That's what makes the column so interesting."

The boy's face remained happy and animated, although he said nothing.

"There are still many sides to you, Mark Edwards," Mari said.

"A front and a back," I said.

Mari said, "From your column, I'd say you still suffer from as many conflicts as there are in the textbooks. Even some which haven't been diagnosed yet."

I looked from Clark to Mari.

"What does that mean?"

"It means you're still totally human," she said. "You always were."

"Is that good?"

"Oh, yes," she said.

I said, "I don't know."

"You can't grow without conflicts," Mari said.

Clark laughed and said to her, "You're beginning to sound like Dear Mark Edwards."

"I don't know," I said. "To me, this whole world is suffering one huge identity crisis, everyone in it, every one of us, maybe caused by the diminution of our institutions, maybe by our incredibly shifting value systems. . . ." I realized I was beginning to sound like Dear Mark Edwards, but the boy, Mari's young man, was looking at me with interest and, goddamnit, was it respect? I laughed. "The big issue of the age is what do you call a prostitute—in this thoroughly promiscuous world. There's no bigger issue. No one knows who he is, or how he fits in."

"You don't call a prostitute," Clark said. "You come to her."

And that, I thought, came from a gigolo!

"By the way, Mark," Mari said. By the way of what, after twenty-one years? "If you ever need a good lawyer, I've got a hell of a fellow here in town. Name of Roberts."

Marvelous Mari of the violet eyes.

"Tell me something, Mari."

"Anything."

"Do you have any stationery? I mean, the pretty kind, engraved or whatever?"

"No." She smiled. "I have never succeeded in buying stationery."

Her violet eyes.

"I'll be right back." I stood up, but I was not going off to a hotel, this time. The city sewers were summoning my baseball beer. "I'll be right back."

After I was in the men's room, I heard someone else enter. Clark was washing his hands.

. . . *if the young man is as attractive as you say* . . . I had written "Senior Officer" . . . *he is used to the sexual tensions around him and will be able to handle you more deftly than you expect.* . . .

I had been such a young man, once.

Washing my hands two basins away, I said, "What's your last name, Clark?"

"Edwards."

Jesus!

My stomach, my whole spine, my shoulders lurched.

Drying his hands, looking at me, he said, again, "Edwards."

Tossing the balled-up paper towel into the wastebasket—a perfect shot—he said, "You're my father."

He stood there, surrounded by white tile, truly emerged from nowhere, arms at his side, feet sort of together, informally presenting himself, that happy, self-confident expression on his face, a young lion as sure of this territory he had just claimed for himself as he was of any other.

Jesus.

Wrongly, I did not want him to see the wetness in my eyes, so, rightly, I grabbed him to me and hugged him, cheek to cheek, shoulder to shoulder.

We were laughing/whooping, of course, my son and I.

Clark Edwards.

"I've heard about these incidents in men's rooms," I said.

Above his smile, his eyes were wet, too.

I walked down the room, away from him, and turned, and then just slumped against a basin.

"How you must hate me," I said.

"Why?" He was still standing on his own feet, arms at his side. "You never knew I existed," he said. "I just saw that."

"You knew I exist?"

"Of course!" He laughed. "Your code name is the Three B's—big, beautiful, and baseball. She always talks about you. She loves you. So do I."

"You do?"

"Of course."

"I've never done anything for you."

"You've given me life," he said. "And I like life." He shrugged. "Other than that, you've never done anything against me."

We laughed.

"Gimme a chance," I said.

"I will."

I was able to change the position of my feet on the floor.

"How did you grow up?" I asked. How did you grow up without me? That didn't work. "What kind of a life have you had?"

"Terrific. With Mari. Paris. London. Not in this country too much. Not too many schools. She wanted to be a teacher, you know. Zorn."

"What's Zorn?"

"A little place in Switzerland. We have a chalet, go skiing there. There's a farm outside Paris—"

"But how have you lived?"

"Lots of love. Lots of sex. Milk. Fresh eggs. Music. The whole bit."

"Life with Mari."

"Who could beat it?"

"No one, I guess."

"Mari makes money," Clark said. "And she enjoys it. She gives life and substance to all her dreams."

"She gave you the name Clark Edwards."

"Someone did."

"And she buys out a whole box on the first base line on my birthday."

"Oh, yeah. Happy birthday. You look okay for forty."

"Thanks."

"I mean it. Really okay."

I washed my face, dried my hands, finally, put my hand on Clark's, my son's, shoulder, and said, "Let's go find Mari."

The dining room was totally empty.

"She's gone," I said.

"I knew she would be. When she ordered the crab meat salad. She hates crab meat." Clark sat in Mari's seat and I in mine. "That was a signal to me," he said. "Attack!"

I said, "She always was quietly spectacular in her exits."

Clark said, "The second baseman, today, Fred Jennings, didn't he sort of invade the shortstop's territory when he caught that fly?"

"No," I said. "Look, Krebs moved over, on purpose, to get out of Jennings' way, you see, so Jennings could make the catch and tag the guy coming in from first, that was understood."

"That guy," Clark said, "who writes baseball for your newspaper, Buzz Hodd? Is he any good?"

"Do you think so?"

Clark Edwards was sprawled long on the straight-backed chair, arms folded across his chest.

He said, "I think he stinks."

Could Mari have written his lines for him?

Not even Mari could have written his lines for him.

"I don't know all that much about baseball, it's hard to follow just from the Paris *Tribune*. . . ."

We talked until nine-thirty (I left a one-hundred-dollar tip for the long use of the table at Saunders'). Clark had to go to the club then, Mari's club. He plays the guitar there or something.

I gave him directions to the Island house.

Mari and he are coming out tomorrow (now today; my birthday is over) for a picnic on the beach. I'll get the picnic stuff first thing in the morning.

No crab meat!

I've had enough of Mari's disappearing trick.

She does it too well.

We'll use these sacks (now five of them) of telegrams, birthday wishes and vituperation, for kindling for the fire for the hot dogs. They might get a kick out of that.

Surprises.

All on my birthday.

Sometime before this vacation is over I might even tell that kid, Clark Edwards, everything there is to know about airport fires—straight from the mouth of a man who's been to one (1).

(August 3)

Dear Mark Edwards:

Last April, I wrote you that I had discovered the man I had been married to, for a short while, a long time ago, is living in the same city I'm living in, and you wrote me back, in your column, saying "Sometimes it is best to leave memories alone—as memories."

I'm sure you were right, in general, but in this case you couldn't have been more wrong!

By accident, we met in a line outside a movie theater and, instead of seeing the movie, went to have something to eat together.

It was marvelous! I was so glad to see him.

Old Friend

Dear Old Friend:
Love Never Faileth.

Dear Mark Edwards:
I love Timmy more than life itself, and I have all year, I've told him so enough times, and all he does is laugh at me, especially when he's with his friends.
I'm going to keep loving him, I can't help it, but will he ever stop laughing at me?

Scorned

Dear Scorned:
Love Never Faileth.

Dear Mark Edwards:
I knew when I married him my husband liked to gamble, and I enjoyed playing cards and going to the race track and ball games with him, but after a while it dawned on me he's compulsive. He admits it. He's joined Gamblers Anonymous and I've taken a job to pay for his psychiatry (my salary goes straight from the store to the psychiatrist) and he is trying, but I hate seeing him so miserable. What can I do to make his daily life happier?

Queen of Hearts

Dear Queen of Hearts:
Love Never Faileth.

Dear Mark Edwards:
My wife has become so liberated, everything—getting dinner, making love, going shopping, vacuuming the rug—everything is "a negotiation."
It takes more time and energy to negotiate who does what when where how and why than it takes to do whatever-the-hell-it-is we're negotiating!
I don't see the fun in this.

The Reluctant Clarence Darrow

Dear Reluctant Clarence Darrow:
Love Never Faileth.

14.

July 25

Dear Mark Edwards:

I read your column once in a while (when it's in the news-paper near the sport pages) and I always end up shaking my head over how you can write such shit.

Man, what you write is nowhere near where it's at.

In this world, man, there are poor folks—people who never can get enough to eat, from the beginning of their life to their end.

Men and women who can't get jobs to keep up their families and their pride, because they're black.

Indians, who are born into concentration camps called "Reservations" and live their lives there, and die there.

Where's your head?

All you write about is people gettin' it off with each other, women who have fun beatin' on their husbands, chicks whose cunts are so big they can't get no satisfaction between their legs, what the fuck you're supposed to call meatbox mamas—shit like that.

Come on, will you, put out with a little sense.

Everett Lamb, Jr.

August 3

Dear Mr. Lamb:

I agree with you, and what you say bothers me.

There are two Big Truths we're dealing with here.

The first is I'm not black, not Indian, and my poverty, I guess, has been only relative.

The second truth is, I don't get letters from the poor, blacks, and Indians.

People excluded by Society from birth never feel they have the right to use any of Society's forms—even a stupid column like mine—to express themselves.

That's the real tragedy.

Believe me, I'll run such letters if I ever get them.

Love Never Faileth,
Mark Edwards

July 28

Dear Mark Edwards:

I have this mad desire to write you a letter.

So I have.

Janey Hillis

August 3

Dear Janey:

I have the same mad desire to answer you.

So I have.

Love Never Faileth,
Mark Edwards

July 27

Dear Mark Edwards:

Me and some of my cell block partners want you to know just how bad things are here at Covey Prison, because we don't want to riot or nothin' like that. Certain numbers would just end up doin' more time.

First of all, there are supposed to be two men to a cell here at Covey, that's the way the place was built, and in my cell there are five men, all using the same shit bowl. I'm in for six to ten years and for two and a half years now I've been sleeping on a thin mattress on the cold floor.

There's no rehabilitation project here, only a chaplain who's a drunk.

There aren't even enough jobs.

Forget about the food. We don't need to tell you about that. Slop unfit for human insumption.

Worst thing is, we petitioned the Old Man several times now just for the right to clean this place up ourselves, paint a few walls, wash the windows, you know what he says?

He says, "No, conditions is too overcrowded for that."

How do you like that?

Anyway, we thought you should know.

The Insiders
(Jim Shomer & Friends)

August 3

Dear Jim Shomer & Friends:

Thanks for writing me.

It's bad enough having to spend time inside, I guess, without having to put up with such overcrowded conditions, such filth and slop.

What kind of good is that supposed to be doing you?

After all, you guys aren't responsible for all the crimes in the world.

Love Never Faileth,
Mark Edwards

July 30

Dear Mark Edwards:

What do you do with a husband who's just plain selfish?

He buys plenty clothes for himself.

"Oh, honey," he goes, "you know I just buy the clothes 'cause I have to go to the office every day. I have to dress nice."

I buy one little dress and the shit hits the fan.

We can't afford! I'm spoiled!

How come clothes for him are a necessity and for me a luxury, I want to know?

> The Woman in Rags
> with a Fashion-plate Husband
> (Estelle Ceer)

August 3

Dear Mrs. Ceer:

Why don't you get yourself a job and then you'd have your own excuse to buy clothes?

> Love Never Faileth,
> Mark Edwards

July 27

Dear Mark Edwards:

In your newspaper column you've published many letters from old people who say they're full of life and all that.

I'm not.

I'm just old.

You must never write in your column it's a pleasure being old. It's a terrible thing.

My husband's dead, Ernie of forty-two years married!

All my friends are dead.

No money.

No respect.

Pains everywhere all the time in my neck.

Please don't say it's all right being old. It's not.

> The Old Mrs. M.
> (Mrs. Ernest Chall)

August 3

Dear Mrs. Chall:

You see how easy it is to make a new friend?

You wrote me, and I write you back.

Make a new friend today. Make another new friend tomorrow.

And have the doctor examine your neck, please.

> Love Never Faileth,
> Mark Edwards

August 3

Dear ME:

"That does it," Monroe Lipton, Publisher, said, swinging in his swivel chair, feet off the floor, one hand on his mammoth oak desk: his whole body, not just his head, shaking no, no, no. "That does it. Tears it. Finished. Kaput!"

He put his hands up, palms toward us, to indicate he would not brook dissent.

He said, "No."

I looked at Jim Krikorian, Managing Editor, to see if he knew what Lipton was talking about.

Krikorian knew.

I didn't.

Midafternoon, Lipton had summoned me to his office.

Krikorian was already there.

Neither rose when I entered.

In fact, Krikorian's head descended farther into his open shirt collar.

I filed away some rather nice phrases of greeting I had prepared (like: "It's hot enough to fry an egg on Buzz Hodd's stomach"; "Always nice to come over to this side of the building to visit my money") and sat down quietly.

One really shouldn't join in an argument until one knows what the topic is. (I have noticed that, by the age of forty.)

Lipton picked up today's paper, already opened to my column.

" 'Love Never Faileth,' " he said. " 'Love Never Faileth, Love Never Faileth'!"

He slapped the paper with his open hand, as if it had said something naughty.

"Where the hell did you get that?"

"A little ditty I thought up. I think."

"What does it mean?"

"What does it mean? It means—"

"Is that how you intend to write your column from now on? Answer everything with 'Love Never Faileth'? 'Old Friend'? 'Scorned'? 'Queen of Hearts'? 'The Reluctant Clarence Darrow'? I think you're having a nervous breakdown!"

"You're tired, Mark," Jim Krikorian said.

"Tired? I'm just back from vacation. How can I be tired?"

"Crackers," Lipton said. "He's gone bonkers."

"Love Never Faileth," I said.

"Is it true you're getting divorced again?" Jim asked.

I gave a sprightly nod. "Pamela's in Sun Valley now," I said. "It's not a complete waste of time for her. Gives her a chance to finish up her book. *Film Stars I've Spat in the Eye Of* or something."

"Well, maybe you're just upset," Lipton said.

"I'm not upset."

"Anybody would be upset," Jim said.

"Not anybody who's tasted her cooking."

"Look, Mark," Lipton said, in a Calm but Firm Manner, "We're taking over your column." Definite. "You're tired. Upset over this divorce thing. You've been under strain. You can't handle it."

"What are you talking about?"

"The strain," Krikorian said. "Too much."

"You're—I mean, the column runs in two hundred and sixty-five newspapers now. Right, Jim?"

"Two hundred and sixty-five."

"You've done well with it, Mark."

"Prostitutes are on strike coast to coast," Krikorian said. "Is that a strike, or a 'shutout'?"

"That puts a strain on other people," I said. "Not me."

"Has the murderer of that broad been found yet?" Lipton asked.

"Silva Mellon?"

"No," Krikorian answered. "He hasn't."

"Then I don't know what good it's all doing. Doubtful publicity value. Look, Mark, we're making a deal with the syndicate."

I said nothing.

"We'll staff the column, and operate it from here. We'll give you 10 percent of the gross for the continued use of the name Mark Edwards."

"You can live comfortably on 10 percent of the gross, Mark," Jim Krikorian said. "The Florida Keys. Baja California. Drink beer in the afternoons."

"You could even get another job," Lipton offered. "As long as you don't write under the name Mark Edwards, of course."

"In fact . . ." Krikorian said.

"In fact," Lipton said, "we'll give you 25 percent of the net if you change your name altogether. Legally. I mean, go into court, change your name. Go live in some other part of the world. We'd see you got your money regularly."

"You'd be rich," Jim said. "I wish Monroe would offer me the same deal."

The message: Please go away.

If I have to hear it so often, it should be set to music.

Rather calmly, under the circumstances, I think, I said, "What makes you guys think you can do this?"

"Well," Lipton said, "we have a half interest in the column. . . ."

"Originally, the column was copyrighted in this newspaper," Krikorian added.

"My name first appeared on my birth certificate."

"And we're a big, powerful city newspaper," Monroe Lipton said. "And, basically, you're a little shit."

"The Syndicate will do pretty much as we ask," Krikorian said. "We buy lots of stuff from them."

"So that's what we're going to do," Monroe Lipton said. "Thought we'd do you the courtesy of telling you in person."

"You can't do this," I said, having stood up and staggered to the door.

I turned and shook my fist at the oak desk.

"I know who I am and what I am. I'm Mark Edwards, and there ain't no others!"

"Sure there are," Lipton said. "There are lots of others."

So, red-faced, blood pounding in my ears, I walked down the corridor to the city room door, turned on my heel and walked back and confronted Jim Krikorian.

"What are you trying to do to me?" I asked.

"Wise guy. 'Love Never Faileth.' That did it."

"Lipton's trying to steal the column. From pure greed."

"Why not?"

"Why not? Jim!"

"How do you think you got the column in the first place?"

"Tell me."

"Your wife."

"What?"

"Pamela and I are old friends. Didn't you know that?"

"Not really. I guess I didn't."

"She and I had lunch together. Sometime last winter. She asked me if I could upgrade your job, somehow. So you'd feel better about yourself. I mean, in bed with Pamela Jensen, film critic for *Hawthorne's*. Somethin'. She hasn't been, frankly, very pleased with me about it. The way things worked out. If you get me."

Staring at him, I felt there was enough room between my eyeballs and their sockets to swing a baseball bat.

"It was I who thought up the precise nature of the column," Jim Krikorian said. "Who owes you anything?"

Finding myself swaying forward, I took a step in that direction, found that balanced nicely, so took another one, and another one, and after what seemed an hour or two, found myself several meters down the corridor from Krikorian. Managing Editor.

"Where are you going?" he asked.

"Do a column," I said. "Doncha know I'm a pro?"

(August 4)

Dear Mark Edwards:

My Mommy and Daddy are getting a divorce and they say I should understand it, but I don't.

Ricky

Dear Ricky:

Some things take a long time to understand, but, sooner or later, everything is understandable.

Dear Mark Edwards:

We want you to know just how bad things are here at Covey Prison. There's no rehabilitation project here. There aren't enough jobs. The food is slop.

There are supposed to be two men in a cell. In my cell there are five.

When we asked the Warden if we could clean this place up ourselves, paint a few walls, wash the windows, he said, "No, conditions are too crowded for that."

The Insiders

Dear Insiders:

I think any Society that makes its prisoners live like that is criminal.

Dear Mark Edwards:
Ernie, my husband of 42 years, is dead.
All my friends are dead.
Please don't say it's all right being old. It's not.
It's terrible.

The Old Mrs. M.

Dear Mrs. M.:
Make a new friend today.
Make another new friend tomorrow.
By the end of the week, all your friends won't be dead.

Dear Mark Edwards:
My husband buys plenty of clothes for himself, because, he says, he has to go to the office every day.
But he yells and hollers I'm spoiled if I buy one little dress for myself!

The Woman in Rags

Dear Woman in Rags:
Why don't you buy your husband his clothes?
Maybe, to get you to stop, he'll let you buy some for yourself.

DEAR READER:
Mark Edwards receives very few, if any, letters reporting specific incidents and issues from members of minority groups. This column belongs to everyone. We'd like to hear from you.

15.

Dear ME:

The place was crowded, which I would not expect on an August night.

Standing behind the velvet rope this side of the brilliant spotlight at the entrance to the main room, I had difficulty getting the eye of the headwaiter, a short man in black tie and patent leather shoes.

Instantly he had disdained me with a flick of his eye through the bright light: me, a forty-year-old man, alone, probably in town on business trying to purge in one night the virtue banked in a hundred nights at home with the family.

Patiently I kept waggling to him and, finally, patiently, he came over to me.

"I'm Mark Edwards," I said. "News/Features Syndicate."

The shock in his face was considerable.

The velvet rope was dropped as if he wished I'd never seen it. I was led into the blinding light at the entrance.

"One moment, Mr. Edwards. We'll set up a table for you."

And when he said "set up," he meant *set up*. Not just scrape the tablecloth and empty the ashtray.

As he conducted his staff with leaping eyebrows and snapping fingers, a table was rushed across my path on somebody's head, chairs on two other people's heads. Dimly through the dark outside my light-bath, I watched them "set up" the table in front of all the others, at the edge of the dance floor. Other tables in the area, with people at them, were gently, firmly shoved aside. A cloth and an ashtray established the table in its place.

"Mr. Edwards?"

Regret was in the headwaiter's eye that I had had to stand for a full minute and witness such labor.

I sat at the table, blinking to adjust my eyes to the nightclub light, feeling the resentment and curiosity of everyone around me.

"May I bring you a drink, Mr. Edwards?" the headwaiter asked.

I wanted to say beer. In memory of the old days. Memories that were not best left alone—as memories. Of when I would go to the cocktail lounge and have a beer waiting to walk Mari home. Her shiny green panties and lace bra with tassels dangling from her tits, and those obscene, high-heeled shoes. I wanted a beer.

"Bring me a beer," I said.

A small orchestra was playing on a platform and people, dressed in the height of fashion, were dancing. Two or three of them were nude. One of the naked girls had a diamond attached, somehow, to the dimple in her left ass-cheek. It played with the light most beguilingly as she danced.

(I am very grateful to this diary. Dear ME. I am convinced it has helped me from going bananas. Apples, pears, nuts, and rutabagas as well. Certainly, sitting at that table, awakening slowly, stupidly to the ambience of Mari's, I had not adjusted, at all, to the shock of the conversation I had had a few hours earlier with Monroe Lipton and Jim Krikorian. *Who owes you anything?* Who indeed? Only now, writing this in the airport lounge, waiting for the airplane that will take me far away, *by* writing this, am I beginning to adjust to what has happened since.)

The girl who brought me my beer was gorgeous.

Mari had created a most fanciful environment.

Except for two areas, the small, low platform-stage and the brightly lit entrance, the murals on the wall were cycloramic, a narrative history of universal sexual fantasies, from the beginning of time to now, whenever that is, from left to right, indicated, sketched more than fully executed, leaving plenty for the viewer to fill in, dream on, imagine, create, contribute, seeming to emerge from the wall itself, depending upon the light, as you looked, as such things do come and go from our subconsciousness, both the sacred and profane, the divine and the bestial. A young, fully blooming Adam and Eve. A naked Europa astride the Bull. The Roman athlete, graceful and noble in his perfection. A foot with rawhide laced up its calf. A Carmen-like slut in a window frame, her breasts on the sill. A string of naked women, in chains. Figures dancing, wildly, as you'd discern them on the side of a teacup. Top-hatted and gowned figures at a lawn party, or in a park. Full-lipped, full-breasted Polynesians, charming in their innocent stare. The foot again, now in a jackboot. Two youngsters, sitting on a beach, as you would see them today, tonight, nearly but not entirely naked, looking oddly burdened, yet, still, with all juvenescence in their eyes.

The platform began to revolve slowly, the orchestra still playing. The dancers led the applause and took their seats.

The next quarter of the stage to be seen held nothing but a big, rumpled brass bed, bathed in light.

And that received great applause.

The third quarter of the stage, as it revolved into view, revealed my son, Clark Edwards, standing/sitting, leaning against a tall stool, his head down, eyes fixed on his guitar, the lights sparkling on his hair, his shoulders, his forearms, his thighs, as he played, played superbly something I identified as Fado, profound in its relentless anguish, profound in its relentless vitality. A boy, a beautiful young man, and his guitar.

And he received great applause.

As I sat there, dumb with love for him.

. . . you must hate me.

Why? . . . You've given me life. And I like life.

While he was being applauded, cheered, loved, still seeming to pay attention only to his guitar, he hit four simple, childlike chords, down the scale, played them again, in more of a walking beat, and, as the stage began to revolve again, taking him off, he strummed again, this time the orchestra backstage rising with a combination of sounds that made me think of a donkey dancing on a music box, and from all around us came a chorus of young, playground voices singing *La la di da, la di da, la di da, da, da . . . !* so that the last time he strummed the four chords on stage we were completely immersed in this music, this beat.

The third quarter of the stage locked into place, empty.

There was wild screaming and applause and stamping of feet. People near the main entrance to the room were standing, craning to see. Some were applauding over their heads. One man stood on a chair.

There, in the bright light of the entrance, dressed in a shiny, white, one-piece pantsuit, microphone casually held in her hand, was Mari. Magnificent Mari. Smiling.

La la di da, la di da, da, da . . . !

The music, the chorus rose, as did the applause.

Seemingly taking her time, but exactly on beat, Mari brought the microphone near her mouth and, remaining there in the bright light of the entrance so most of the room could hear her but not see her, she sang:

> *Well, you know that I'm not a gambler*
> *But I'm bein' gambled on.*
> *They put in a nickel*
> *And I sing a little song.*

Walking a little behind the beat, *La la di da, la di da, da, da,* spotlight on her, the room shaking with applause as she came into everybody's view, she attained the middle of the dance floor (she never did go up onto her stage), the middle of the light, and turned, and sang to us.

> *Well, I don't mind that they're lucky,*
> *But it seems like they always win*
> *And gambling is illegal*
> *In the state of mind I'm in.*

Waist gathered, legs flared, the smooth, hard material shining in the light like something that had never, could never have existed before, unzipped to her navel, her skin heartbreaking in its invitation to Mari's world, violet eyes rare in their isolation, with joy, feet firmly planted against the music: the street urchin, cognizant of the Eternal. Nevertheless, still joyful in her being, offering, giving a moment of that being, a vision, a song to any passerby.

> *And if I had a nickel*
> *For each time that I've been put on*
> *I would be the Nickel Man*
> *And I'd sing the nickel song.*

The audience sang with the chorus, *La la di da, la di da, da, da!*, while Mari fluted over them. It was like a revival meeting or a political rally or both.

> *They put in a nickel*
> *And I sing a little song.*
> *. . . They're only puttin' in a nickel,*
> *And they want a dollar song!*

From backstage, with the orchestra, maybe a little louder, more leading than it should have been, strode the virility of Clark's guitar, a kid, a nice son, walking with his mother, walking his mother on.

> *Well, you know I don't know so many things,*
> *But I know what's been goin' on:*
> *We're only puttin' in a little*
> *To get rid of a lot that's wrong!*

Despite my prominent seat, at no point had Mari looked at me.

You've never come.

How do you know?

I'd know.

It was fun, I thought, watching her, without her knowing I was there.

> *And if we had a nickel*
> *For each time that we've been put on*
> *We'd all be the Nickel Man*
> *And we'd sing the nickel song!*

The people loved Mari so much they had no intention of letting her finish.

The audience was on its feet (many standing on chairs; one girl stood on a table).

A man, an older man, at the table next to mine, had tears rolling down his cheeks.

> *You know, they're only puttin' in a nickel,*
> *And they want a dollar song!*

In the center of the light, in the center of the dance floor, the music continuing, Mari extended her hand to my table.

Could she see me through the light?

I didn't move.

La la di da, la di da, da, da!

She came closer to me, held her hand within my reach, and said, so only I could hear her: "Come on, man I love."

She led me to the center of the dance floor, the center of the light and, holding my hand, waited for the audience's curiosity to quiet them a little.

Then she said into the hand microphone, "Friends—I want you to meet the man I've always loved—my husband of twenty-one years—and someone you all love very much, too—Mark Edwards!"

Audiences do gasp. (At least, this one did!)

They needed to, for all the cheering they were about to do.

But I said to Mari, "Whaddaya mean, your husband of twenty-one years?"

Holding the microphone out of range, at her side, her violet eyes unworldly in that light, Mari said, "I never divorced you."

"Jesus Christ!"

"That's why I thought you'd need a lawyer," she said.

"Jesus! I'm a bigamist? I've been a bigamist all these years?"

"No longer," she said. "I just talked to Pamela in Sun Valley. Your divorce came through two hours ago."

La la di da, la di da, da, da!

Someone in the audience—a man's voice—shouted, "Thank you, Mark Edwards!"

"Who's that?" I said into the noise. "Jumbo Dondershine?"

The guitar strode heavily again, with the orchestra, with the chorus, and, holding my hand, Mari sang:

> *And if we had a nickel*
> *For each time that we've been put on*
> *We'd all be the Nickel Man*
> *And we'd sing the nickel song!*

La la di da, la di da, da, da!

And someone took the microphone and I had Mari in my arms and we were dancing, *La la di da, la di da, da, da!* and I said, "Mari, may I reenter your fantasy?" and Mari said, "You've never left it, Mark."

Jake Roberts, Mari's lawyer, was upstairs in the living room of Mari's apartment when we arrived (at three-thirty in the morning), comfortable in the divan, his feet up on the coffee table, working on papers from a briefcase.

"Everything's set, Mari, for you and Clark to leave in the morning. The final papers are all here."

He held up a manila envelope.

Mari said to me, "Clark and I are going over to France today. Have to be there for a closing. You know. We've needed to buy another perfume factory. This one's in Orléans. You're coming with us, aren't you?"

"I don't know."

"Can't you do the column anywhere?"

"Anywhere there's a post office."

"We usually try to spend most of August on the farm outside Paris. Oh, yeah, Jake, Mark thinks he has a legal problem."

She hadn't introduced us.

"Congratulations on your divorce," Jake said. "As you became better known, Mari and I were afraid—"

"It didn't happen," Mari said. "But now they want to take the column away from him."

Jake grinned at me. "And you don't want them to?"

I said, "I'm just getting good at it."

"Mark will explain it to you," Mari said. "I'm going to take a bath."

So I told Jake Roberts my tale until four o'clock in the morning, and he listened, and finally, then, slapped his briefcase closed and reached for his shoes and reached for his jacket, saying, "Forget about it. I'll take care of it. Move physically, immediately, out of your office, the newspaper office—this morning—and establish some other business address. Then go to France, if you want to, and keep writing the column."

"What are you going to do?"

"Renegotiate with the Syndicate."

"How can you? I mean, the newspaper, Monroe Lipton—"

"Fuck the newspaper. One newspaper out of what? Two hundred and sixty-five? You're Mark Edwards. Didn't you know that?"

"I'm just discovering."

"Give 'em a few points, if you want. Want to give 'em 3 percent of net? For old times' sake?"

"No," I said. "Too much shit under the bridge."

So, early this morning, in bed with my wife of twenty-one years (after twenty-one years), two people, when love is young, when love is old, *each of us beautiful,* she said, as if she'd never said it before, after so little, after so much, loving each other and again:

"Mari," I said, looking up at us in the mirror on the ceiling above her bed, "a question. I mean this as a question—not as a jab in the ribs. You loved me. You love me. What happened? What came ahead of me? Ambition? Money?"

Her violet eyes against the field-green sheets looked at me in the mirror, and looked down somewhere, maybe at the top of the door across the room.

"No. Life," she said. "Rising up." She glanced at me in the mirror. "I'm trying to answer you, Mark. Why I left you. Being came before loving. One must be, to love. Is that an answer? One must be, as well as love. Does that make any sense?"

I haven't slept since.

Rapidly, I moved out of the newspaper office this morning (telling Ms. Halamay I was fed up with the air conditioner's never working properly) into a nice little office appropriately situated in a building full of dentists, orthodontists, psychiatrists, hairdressers and one (1) bookie who says his specialty is speedy baseball results, tacked together a couple of columns for News/Features Syndicate, and then went to the airport, where I've been writing dear me.

The departure of my flight is being announced.

Clark and Mari said they'd meet me at the airport in Paris, in the morning.

(August 21)

Dear Mark Edwards:
So Silva Mellon was murdered, not by the fuzz, not by a pimp, but by Cissy, her own girlfriend-lover!
It had nothing to do with her trying to organize us body entertainers. And the big strike was all for nothing!
Ain't that the pits?
From now on, you can call us Stupid.

The Stupids

Dear Bawdy Entertainers:
History, I've noticed, has a way of being inconclusive.

Dear Mark Edwards:
Would you believe I got back a term paper on which my Psychology professor had written, "Your work has improved *alot*"?

A—/B+

Dear A—/B+:
Yes.

Dear Mark Edwards:
I've got five children to feed here on the money from the State and

these people who make the cheap food cereals, like that, keep putting up their prices something wicked.

Don't they have any mercy at all?

Mama No Way

Dear Mama No Way:

Your food dollar can go further if you buy raw, fresh vegetables and fruits, in season. It means more shopping and cooking for you, but, remember, when you buy packaged foods a good part of your food money goes to pay for the package.

Dear Mark Edwards:

My girl friend is very shy about herself, always wearing this old Army jacket and long corduroy pants and this floppy hat she says she's crazy about.

She's really got a good bod (I think), but I can't get her to believe It and relax a little.

Rap-up's Boyfriend

Dear Rap-up's Boyfriend:

Love Never Faileth.

Dear Mark Edwards:

I would like to know what is the personal effect upon you of writing the "Dear Mark Edwards" column.

Friendly Doc

Dear Friendly Doc:

It's mutual.